BOOK ONE: YESTERMORROW

Accelerated Reader
Level 4.7

TIMETRIPPER

BOOK ONE: YESTERMORROW

STEFAN PETRUCHA

razOr
bill

Timetripper 1: Yestermorrow

RAZORBILL

Published by the Penguin Group
Penguin Young Readers Group
345 Hudson Street, New York, New York 10014, U.S.A.
Penguin Group (USA) Inc., 375 Hudson Street, New York, New York 10014,
U.S.A.
Penguin Group (Canada), 90 Eglinton Avenue, Suite 700, Toronto, Ontario,
Canada M4P 2Y3 (a division of Pearson Penguin Canada Inc.)
Penguin Books Ltd, 80 Strand, London WC2R 0RL, England
Penguin Ireland, 25 St Stephen's Green, Dublin 2, Ireland
(a division of Penguin Books Ltd)
Penguin Group (Australia), 250 Camberwell Road, Camberwell, Victoria 3124,
Australia (a division of Pearson Australia Group Pty Ltd)
Penguin Books India Pvt Ltd, 11 Community Centre, Panchsheel Park, New
Delhi – 110 017, India
Penguin Group (NZ), Cnr Airborne and Rosedale Roads, Albany, Auckland 1310,
New Zealand (a division of Pearson New Zealand Ltd)
Penguin Books (South Africa) (Pty) Ltd, 24 Sturdee Avenue, Rosebank,
Johannesburg 2196, South Africa

Penguin Books Ltd, Registered Offices: 80 Strand, London WC2R 0RL, England

10 9 8 7 6 5 4 3 2 1

Library of Congress Cataloging-in-Publication Data

Petrucha, Stefan.
  Yestermorrow / Stefan Petrucha.
    p. cm. — (Timetripper ; bk. 1)
  Summary: Teenager and genius Harry Keller discovers an alternate dimension
he calls "A-Time," in which he can see and affect events in the past, present, and
future.
  ISBN 1-59514-076-X
  [1. Space and time—Fiction. 2. Time travel—Fiction.] I. Title.
  PZ7.P44727Yes 2006
  [Fic]—dc22

                                                                    2005023833

Printed in the United States of America

For Tom Sutton
(1937–2002)

The intuitive mind is a sacred gift and the rational mind is a faithful servant. We have created a society that honors the servant and has forgotten the gift.

—ALBERT EINSTEIN

1. The clock was seriously unhelpful. *Tick. Tick. Tick* was all it said, but what it meant was that poetry class was coming, that it was getting closer and closer.

Shifting in her seat and grinding her teeth, Siara Warner struggled to turn the dull, stupid clock into something poignant and meaningful, something she could write a poem about. An enthralling poem. An exciting poem. A poem she'd have to read aloud in class in *twenty minutes*. She'd already given up on the extra-credit assignment, describing someone in a single word. Now she had to finish the poem, or she'd have a single word for herself: *screwed*.

Eyeing the lurching second hand, she tried to force great thoughts into her head: *Maybe it's like a long, thin bug trying to shudder free of its body or like that Greek guy Mr. Elenko talked about last week in lit. What's his name? Emphasis? Psoriasis? No. Sisyphus. Yeah, I can see it: the second hand is a rock pushed up a hill, from six to twelve, then it falls, twelve to six, then it gets pushed back up, six to twelve, forever. Probably feels trapped. It*

1

must feel trapped. Maybe it's dying to stop circling, to crack the plastic cover, zip out all over the place and make wild zigzag patterns on the walls. Then no one will ever get to class again.

No use. The clock was non-poetic, if that was a word. Maybe it was a-poetic, like amoral, asymmetric, or a-pain-in-the-ass. *Tick. Tick. Tick.*

She blew a puff of air to dislodge some plum-red hairs from in front of her right eye. She'd dyed a few strands last week, thinking it'd be a cool counterpoint to the rest of her long, dirt-brown hair, but now the hairs had a different texture, like half-dried papier-mâché. They were always flopping into her eyes, trying to blind her.

She looked around. During fourth-period study hall, the cavernous plaster box otherwise known as the Robert A. Wilson High School auditorium positively hummed. More than a hundred students read, wrote, and tapped pencils to the tune of earbud-muffled MP3s. They all seemed so happy, so productive, so utterly annoying.

No fair. She'd skipped lunch to be here. She could have been checking out Jasmine's new jeans, listening to Dree talk downloads and uplinks, or going wide-eyed at Hutch's latest antisocial outrage. Instead she'd holed herself away in here so that she could concentrate. And what did she get? Nada. Where was the mad-eyed poet Ms. Tarina promised lurked inside them all?

She picked up her pen, wrote, *Detached*, on a new

line, then slashed it out with a series of blue lines.

Her father was too smart to say so out loud, but he thought poetry was a waste. Twenty-five years as a subway engineer and he wanted a big payoff. With a plasma TV out of the question, having a doctor or a lawyer for a daughter would have to do. Mom just echoed him—and whenever Siara tried to explain how she wanted to write poetry, she could feel their whole bodies wince. She knew they'd hoped that particular conversation was over when she was rejected from the Miramet High School of Art and Design, which had a great writing program. As Siara tried to dredge her soul but came up blank, she was starting to think maybe they were right. Maybe it was over.

She glanced around the room again, hoping she'd somehow missed something incredibly inspiring. Who was in here anyway? You were lucky if you knew ten people in study hall at RAW.

One face she recognized—Todd Penderwhistle's. It wasn't really his face that stood out, though, as much as his door-wide body, long black coat, and shaved head. And, of course, the missing two fingers from his left hand. Some people said that he'd lost them during a knife fight. If she had to sum Todd up in a word, it'd be—*splintery wood*. No, wait. That was two words.

She slumped back and glared at her half page of scribbled lines. This assignment was sticking in her throat like a spear of raw asparagus. Raw, raw, raw.

Robert A. Wilson High School. R. A. W.

Some of these kids traveled up to two hours, by subway and bus, through urban sprawl, just to get to a place she didn't even want to be. It was supposedly one of the best high schools in the country, next to Bronx Science or Brooklyn Tech. Just her luck that testing always came easy to her—Siara was one of three students from her middle school who'd passed the RAW entrance exam. The only test she'd ever failed was the one for Miramet. They required an art portfolio, and Siara couldn't draw to save her life. She wondered if she was the only student here who thought of RAW as her second choice.

And if it was so tough, how had Todd gotten in? Rumor was he'd cheated.

She wrote down two more words, *hopeless munitions*, then crossed them out.

Could she catch up with the others? Maybe Hutch could help with her poem, or at least the excuse for why it wasn't ready. Hutch was good with that kind of stuff. Not Siara.

She was ready to just give up and take off when a tallish thin guy, head down and muttering to himself, made his way down the aisle. Something seemed familiar about him, but his dark hair hung in front of his face, obscuring her view.

The long hair didn't seem like a fashion statement; it was just plain old sloppy, like the rest of him. T-shirt half untucked, buttons undone on the worn flannel shirt he had on over that, an untied sneaker lace. If she had to describe him in a word, it would be *un*. Only that wasn't even a word. Half credit for half a word?

Siara was ready to dismiss him as a medicated-special-ed-kid-whom-she-should-not-pity-just-because-he-was-different, but her body wasn't in sync with her mind. There was definitely something about this guy. . . . Looking at him gave her that weird feeling in her stomach, the fluttery jitters that usually came when she was around a guy she liked. But the mentally challenged were definitely not her type. So why . . . ?

Then he picked up his head and it all made sense.

Harry Keller. Harry Keller was back.

In middle school, Siara'd had a serious crush on Harry. Even underneath his now-shaggy hair, he still had the same clear, piercing hazel eyes, the same adorable face that had gotten to her back then. Nothing had ever happened between them, since it wasn't long after they started hanging out together that he skipped a grade and started RAW early. They'd been friendly, but not close enough to keep in touch. By the time she caught up with him here, he was all into science and physics and the debate team—not her usual circles. Basically, Harry Keller was the smartest kid in a school full of geniuses.

Last year, anyway. Now he really was in special ed. Everyone knew the sad, sad story: his mother had died of cancer when he was a kid. Then just this summer, his father had died in a freaky accident, and Harry's brain had done a major wacky—and he'd wound up in a psychiatric hospital, on medication, the works. She'd thought of sending him a note or a card when she heard about his dad, but they didn't really know each other anymore.

But here he was. And, she remembered, he knew poetry. Once he'd stunned a fourth-grade teacher by reciting an entire speech from some Shakespeare play.

"Hi, Harry," she said, a little too loud.

His eyes shot sideways toward her, brown-green circles visible through hanging locks of hair. She remembered how he'd always had a way of looking at her with his *entire* attention, as if she were the only thing in the world.

"Siara Warner," he answered quietly, as if assigning her a location in his brain. She liked the way he said it.

She smiled back in "friendly" mode, trying her best not to look too pitying.

"How *are* you?" she asked.

He shrugged and managed a slight upward twist to his lips that almost looked like a grin.

"Where are you living now?" she said, pushing forward.

"Still in Brenton, but near Lydig, with my aunt," he said. "It's not so bad."

After a silence, it occurred to her he was waiting for her to say something else.

"Um . . . I'm working on a poem for class. . . ."

"Cool." His hand came forward, the long fingers shaking a little. Siara assumed it was from some medication he was still taking. "Can I see?" he asked.

Pretending to be indecisive, she bobbed her head, then handed him the notebook. Harry would be okay, she told herself. He'd be too terrified to say anything bad.

His eyes danced across the words, not moving left to right, but curving around, up and down, in sweeps. She'd never seen anyone read that way or so quickly. Briefly, she worried he might read it out loud, but Harry's lips didn't move. It didn't matter; she had it memorized:

Alligator, alligator, humpback whale,
These are the things that I see when I sail
Far away to quiet island
I go there when I'm laughing
I go there when I cry
I go there just to say hello
I go to say goodbye
Ripened, stiffened, hardened by the breeze
Floating through the open air, clinging to the trees
All the while on quiet island

Silly little thing. She wasn't sure what it meant, other than expressing a general desire to be anyplace but here, anytime but now. She hated it. It was awful.

She hoped he would say it was brilliant.

His head popped up. "Nice," he said. "Really like the part about simple crystal wishes."

Brow creasing. Seeing red. "Friendly" mode off.

"What simple crystal wishes? There are no simple crystal wishes," Siara said coldly.

He snapped his attention back to the page. Not looking up at her, he handed the notebook back, hand shaking a little more. Was he afraid of *her*?

"Um . . . sorry," he said. "Sorry. You're right."

She was about to feel bad about snapping at him until he added, "But there will be."

What's that *supposed to mean?*

"Look, I really have to get this done in ten minutes," she said, turning back to her work. She assumed her dismissive tone would send him scurrying.

"*Have* to?" he said, in a low voice. "That doesn't make sense." All of a sudden, he didn't seem nervous anymore. Was he making fun of her? Was the crazy guy making fun of *her*?

Siara narrowed her eyes and tried to pretend she thought *he* was the stupid one. "Yeah. Have to. Poetry class. Next period. Nine and a half minutes."

She pointed at the non-poignant, meaningless clock.

Harry blinked a few times. She thought it was a nervous tic, but on closer inspection it seemed like he was trying to suppress a laugh.

Omigod! He's laughing at me! Maybe not out loud, but what difference does that make?

"What?" she said, voice rising half an octave.

"Well, it's a poem, right? I mean, how can you *have* to write a poem?"

8

"It's an assignment. Homework. Of course I have to. If I don't, it'll affect my grade. Even if I don't care about this stupid class anymore, I care about the grade, about getting into college, premed or prelaw, you know," she said, lying.

He looked puzzled, as if remembering her differently.

"Law? You don't care about the class? About that poem? Didn't you want to be a writer back in Brenton? And why would anyone take poetry if they didn't care about it?" he said. "Did you *have* to?"

All of a sudden, feeling like the only thing in Harry Keller's world was no longer quite so charming. She nearly cut him off in her race to change the subject. "Well, isn't part of life what you *have* to do? Like, the dishes?"

"Wow. Dishes and law school, huh? That's a poem right there. Hmm. How many people, right here, right now, want to be doing what they're doing? Maybe no one. Maybe we've all just been institutionalized for so long, like, since kindergarten, we're afraid of what might happen if we don't do exactly as we're told. A lot of people do that their whole lives, drive themselves nuts getting grades in classes they don't care about, so they can get a job they don't really want, just to buy things that won't make them happy. You could write a whole poem about that. Call it, like . . . 'The American Scream.'"

He chuckled, then seemed disappointed she wasn't laughing too.

"'The American Scream'?" he repeated. "Like 'The American Dream' . . . only screaming? Uh . . . maybe I should go now. . . ."

She wasn't laughing at all. She was glaring.

"Why are *you* here, if you don't *have* to be?"

He looked around as if hoping the question were meant for someone standing next to him. "Me? That's easy. If I didn't show up here, I'd get an express ticket back to the psychiatric hospital, where I'd be put on some major brain-numbing meds. What happens to you if you don't finish your poem?"

"Not so much," Siara admitted. Feeling a little guilty, she added, "Sorry about your dad. I can't imagine what that must feel like."

"Me neither, apparently," he said. "My shrink says I still haven't really dealt with it."

If it was a joke, he didn't laugh.

"Okay. But you're doing better now?"

He blew some air between pursed lips and rolled his eyes. He looked embarrassed but also a little mischievous. "I guess. Doctors, teachers, even my aunt all think I'm . . . you know, that I have emotional challenges. But I don't think so. See, I think . . . Well, it's . . . hard to explain."

She felt another twinge of sympathy for him, even more intense. He was out of place, like her, only much,

much worse. He didn't even have his old home to go back to or any parents to disagree with. His arrogance, which she remembered from middle school, was still there, only now it seemed cracked, with little bits of pain poking through. He seemed desperate for someone to talk to, and there were still seven minutes left until the bell.

"Try me," Siara offered.

"Okay," Harry said. "It requires an open mind, but not so open that your brains fall out." He cleared his throat, rubbed his hands together, and said nothing for a while.

"Harry?" Siara asked.

He shrugged. "I've never done this before, so give me a sec. Okay, ready? Here we go. Everybody's brain is always being hit with sights, sound, tastes, and touches from our senses, right? This goes on 24/7, but at any given moment, there's too much for you to deal with consciously, so the brain has filters, to keep you sane. The filters make you think about some data but stop you from thinking about other data. Stand in the middle of a highway and you won't think about the itch on your back as much as you will about the truck that's about to hit you. Make sense?"

"I guess."

"The thing is, while the truck is headed toward you, you *can't* feel the itch on your back. The filters blind you. Now, in my case, I think the trauma of my

11

father's . . . death damaged my filters. I don't think it means I'm crazy. It's the opposite, really. I'm just seeing more of the whole picture. My brain is doing things I never imagined it could. Sometimes I . . . I . . . well, I can't quite put it into words yet, but it feels like I'm on the verge of making some kind of big breakthrough."

"Have you tried talking to anyone else about this?" Siara said, a little nervous because of the wild look he got in his eyes as he said *breakthrough*.

Harry shrugged again. "Sort of. My shrink thinks I'm narcissistic and delusional, glorifying myself so I can avoid dealing with my grief. I think I'm just less afraid of small things, like that itch, like homework, more afraid of big things, like the truck, or, I dunno, the consequence of . . . time."

"It's nice you can think these things through," she said politely. If she still had any tingly feelings toward him, she wasn't having them right now.

It's also nice you're still seeing a shrink, she thought. *Someone to help you keep tabs on that narcissistic-delusional thing.*

He smiled, a little sadly, probably hearing her well-meant condescension. "Thanks."

She felt awful, like she'd hurt him. She didn't want it to end like that, so she said the first thing that popped into her mind.

"So . . . what's the consequence of time?"

He looked at her like *she* was crazy.

"Death," he said.

He said it as if he were talking to a child. As if he were answering, "Four," to an idiot's question. "Just what *is* two plus two?"

Harry twitched and looked down. With a trip and a shuffle, he made his way down the aisle to find a seat alone.

2.

Death.

The word made Siara's shoulders feel heavy, like she was a character in some horror movie with the crazy killer right behind her, invisible until the moment his blade came down.

Harry was talking about his father. Must have been. Probably didn't even realize it. What was the deal with my poem, though? Is he just so crazy he's reading words that aren't there?

Five minutes to the bell. She could keep writing as she did a slow walk to class, buy herself an extra few minutes, but then it would be judgment time. The consequences of homework.

She forced herself to pick up her pen, determined to write anything that came into her head, preferably anything that rhymed, but—a collective, study-hall-wide gasp made her drop her pen. Everyone around her craned their necks to see.

To see what?

14

There was shouting: "Take that . . . out of your . . . !" was all she could make out.

The student monitor—the title was generally thought of as a goofy honorary—leapt up from his folding seat on the stage, knocking it over. It clattered onto the wooden floor, the volume tripled by the stage acoustics. Everyone grew quiet, so Siara could make out every word.

"I won't ask again, Todd," the monitor said. "Feet down."

Todd. Of course Todd Penderwhistle would have to be at the center of any problem.

Siara looked over and saw that Todd's long legs hung over the seat in front of him. His arms were hooked over the chairs on either side. His dark coat hung open from his shoulders, like leathery bat wings. Though the hall was crowded, he had the whole row, the row behind him, and the row in front all to himself. Siara thought she caught a glimpse of finger stubs on his left hand.

Despite the queasy rush she felt from her heart trying to tear its way out of her chest, she couldn't really blame Todd for putting his feet up. The seats were small for her, and he was at least a foot taller. Folding chairs were stacked alongside the stage to create extra rows for school-wide assemblies. One of those might fit him more comfortably, but people, students, weren't allowed to use them.

The monitor stomped to the edge of the stage as if

15

he were in a play, kicking the fallen chair as he went.

Siara squinted. *Who would actually challenge Todd?*

But when she saw who it was, it made perfect sense. Jeremy Gronson was the RAW alpha male—a senior, an amazing academic (though not quite as amazing as Harry Keller had been), and an athlete. He was the school's star quarterback *and* the new captain of the debate team. His clothes fit so well they looked tailored for him. His sandy hair, clear skin, and perfectly toned body made him look like he'd stepped right off the screen of some prime-time soap. He was going to be president someday, or world dictator. Maybe both. He was so perfect, when she wasn't distracted by how freaking hot he was, Siara wanted to scratch him, just to prove there was blood under his skin.

Ugly words spewed from Todd, his voice rising louder and louder. No one Siara knew had the capacity to *be* that loud or angry. But Todd could. He would've made a great lead singer for a metal band if he could read music. If he could read.

"Very original, Todd. So are you going to move, or am I going to write this up?" Jeremy said. "And you know what that means, don't you?"

Siara didn't know what it meant. She didn't know if Todd knew what it meant, but it sounded really good. It sounded like Todd would *have* to listen. But he didn't. He just kept glaring up at Jeremy on the stage.

Siara scanned the aisles. Where the hell was the

study hall teacher, good old roly-poly Mr. Kaufmann? Off on one of his many carcinogen breaks?

"You are *this* close to getting expelled, Sasquatch. Kicked out. Gone. Working fast food the rest of your life *if* they'll have you. I'd *love* to see it happen. Go ahead. Do something. Anything," Jeremy said. He stuck out his right hand, holding his thumb a fraction of an inch from his index finger.

Todd looked away. Some sort of trick to catch Jeremy off guard?

Jeremy took a step closer to the edge of the stage. "Give me an excuse, man. Get up. Hit me. Or just sit there. It's all the same."

It wasn't a completely suicidal challenge. A bunch of Jeremy's football teammates were in the auditorium. They were tensing already, ready to spring. Todd had probably noticed them too, which explained why he hadn't moved.

Todd snapped his arms forward, maybe hoping Jeremy would flinch. He didn't.

Todd pulled his legs back, slammed his feet onto the floor, and stood, stretching to full King Kong height. He was taller than Jeremy, but not by much. Still, Todd spun, showing Jeremy the long lizard back of his duster. Then he stepped off to find another seat.

The auditorium exhaled. Jeremy turned to pick up his fallen chair. Show over.

Wasn't it?

The sound of two feet slamming helter-skelter into the floor brought Siara's attention away from the stage and back to the aisles, where Harry Keller looked like he'd just tripped over his own legs. He seemed utterly oblivious, like Charlie Chaplin in one of those old silent films, mindlessly wandering through a full-scale riot. Having apparently wandered around the entire hall, he was nearing Siara again. She worried he'd eat up the remaining seconds before class with more freaky death talk but breathed a sigh of relief as he headed for an open seat on the aisle.

Looking down, not around, he reached out to put his hand on the seat back just as Todd Penderwhistle did the same. There they were, a few yards from Siara, touching hands. She gasped. Todd really was missing two fingers. The ring finger was a stub. The pinky looked like a piece of bone jutting out from the flesh.

Harry started, clearly equally surprised by what he'd accidentally touched.

"Harry!" Siara hissed through clenched teeth. He didn't hear.

Finally he noticed Todd's hand under his own. He slowly raised his head to look toward where a face would be on a person of average height but found himself staring at Todd's chest. Craning his neck, he looked farther up and locked eyes with the seriously unhappy creature whose hand he held.

Todd whispered, nodding back toward Jeremy,

"Him, I'm going to shoot. You, I'm just going to kill."

Harry didn't take the hint. He didn't even move his hand. He just kept staring, openmouthed, wide-eyed. Siara was terrified Todd would punch him. Harry looked like a bleeder. Did she have any napkins in her bag?

Todd didn't move his hand either. He also kept staring, waiting for Harry to flinch. But Harry just stood there, frozen. Then, as if Todd caught a glimpse of what Harry was seeing, a look of vulnerability flashed on his face.

As soon as it disappeared, Todd withdrew his hand, then used it to shove Harry backward. Harry flew back a good three feet but somehow remained standing. Ignoring him, Todd plopped himself into the aisle seat and tried to stretch his legs out to the side.

Instead of doing what Siara considered the smart thing, like slinking away and hiding, Harry kept staring at Todd. He strutted up and down the aisle, head twisting to keep Todd in his line of sight. Fortunately for Harry, Todd closed his eyes and started rubbing his temples. But Harry kept up his odd little dance, first getting closer, then racing away.

Clenching her teeth, Siara hissed more than whispered, "Harry! Harry! Get over here now!"

He stopped. Siara was sure he'd heard her. As he came near, she got ready to yank him into a seat next to her, for his own damn good. But he didn't slow down. Instead he ran to the front of the auditorium and grabbed some folding chairs from the pile near the stage. He put one here, another there, a third over there, one sideways, one upside down, and another balanced between them. He stepped back, looked, and rearranged them.

Siara's mouth dropped open. It was like watching a berserk interior decorator. As Harry's movements became more and more frenetic, she worried he was having some kind of delusional fit.

A deep, phlegmy laugh made her look behind her. Todd was watching too. Maybe he'd realized Harry was a few enchiladas short of a combo plate. Now, Siara hoped, he wouldn't have to hurt him.

Unfortunately, Todd's nasty laugh also attracted Jeremy's attention. He turned his cool blue eyes first on Todd, then toward what Todd was laughing at. As he spotted Harry in mid-freak-out, he hopped down from the stage, walked over, and put his hand on one of the chairs Harry was frantically trying to place.

Harry yanked it back, violently. "Back off, Gronson! It has to be *here*!"

Anger flashed on Jeremy's face, but he swallowed it.

"Hey, Keller. Hey. Take it easy. Calm down, dude," Jeremy said.

He put his hand on Harry's shoulder. Harry swatted it away.

"No!" Harry said. "No distractions! It's got to be just right or he'll kill you!" Then he actually dared to jab a finger at a spot on Jeremy's forehead. "Right there. Crack! Dead!"

Looking very confused, Jeremy stepped back and shook his head. This gave Harry just enough time to grab a banana peel from a student in the first row, plop it into the aisle, and position it with a careful swipe of his foot.

As Jeremy again moved toward one of the chairs, it was clear to Siara he was losing his patience. But Harry didn't care. He wrapped himself around the chair, ready to defend it as if it were his cub.

That was it for Jeremy. Unlike Todd, he had no need to hit Harry. He just reached for the cell phone clipped to his belt that probably took great photos and had a little keyboard for IMs—and started dialing the appropriate authorities.

Siara stood, wanting to pull Harry out of there, not understanding why she felt so concerned for him. Maybe she could talk him down.

Too late, even if Jeremy hadn't started dialing. Mr. Kaufmann, his tan sweater pulled taut across his potbelly, had returned. His features instantly melted into his famed what's-going-on-here? face, an expression so extreme it always seemed more appropriate for a sitcom than the real world.

Without even speaking to Harry, Kaufmann called security. Of the ten guards at RAW, two were perpetually stationed at the front entrance, which was right across from the auditorium. Some smart-ass student had nicknamed them Didi and Gogo, after the characters from *Waiting for Godot*, because, like the guys in the play, it always seemed they were hanging around waiting for something that never happened.

They were there in seconds, slamming open the doors as loud as they could, then marching in sync down the aisle. They had this funny walk. Didi bopped up and down as he moved, but Gogo swayed from side to side. Moving together, they looked like a baby's toy, something on wheels with a string. They headed straight for Todd, out of habit.

"No, no! This one!" Kaufmann explained, pointing at Harry. Without skipping a beat, they switched course and grabbed a shrieking Harry as gently as underpaid high school security guards were able.

Siara shivered as they took him. A lump welled in her throat.

"I have to make sure the chairs are right!" he screamed as they half carried him out. "I *have* to."

"You don't *have* to do anything," Siara whispered.

A final, muffled, "Leave it where it is!" was heard beyond the double doors leading to the hall. They swung shut. Silence returned.

Slowly the hollow auditorium refilled with chatter. The clock ticked again.

Death.

If she were really a poet, she should be able to take

advantage of everything she'd just seen. Instead she just felt helpless and sad. If Harry Keller's brain could just go pop! like that, what hope was there for the rest of them?

Jeremy strode over to put the chairs away. As he reached for the first one, he glanced at Todd, whose legs were once again hooked over the seat in front of him. Jeremy's face twisted.

"What did I say about the legs?" he shouted, even angrier than before.

Todd Penderwhistle stood, pulled a gun from the folds of his coat, aimed it at Jeremy's head, and squeezed the trigger.

At the same moment, a freshman with a buzz cut and a denim jacket was walking down the aisle. As Todd rose, the freshman hit the banana peel Harry had left on the floor and flew into one of the folding chairs. That chair hit another, which careened into two chairs, ricocheted into a fourth, then finally sent yet another chair flying directly into Jeremy's abdomen.

Whud!

Slammed in the breadbasket, Jeremy folded, sandy hair a blur as his head flashed forward and down. White stars of plaster exploded from the wall behind him at just the level where his head had been. Todd was about to fire again, but before he could, four of Jeremy's teammates jumped him.

Siara froze—mind, body, and heart. One half of her

brain wanted her to run, to scream, to cry all at once, but the other half just would not cooperate. It saw the whole scene, herself included, as something impossible to believe, something unreal, up on a TV screen made of dots and scan lines, or in a book made of words, or told in the hushed tone of a storyteller sitting by a campfire, whispering the single word:

Death.

For the longest time, as all the other students panicked, screamed, and ran, she just sat there, her gaze shifting from the oddball collection of folding chairs back to the bullet hole in the wall. She barely noticed that Todd, now pinned by four football players and Mr. Kaufmann, wasn't fighting back. He was staring as well, his expression every bit as puzzled as her own.

3. As Didi and Gogo half dragged Harry down the hall, his brain was a beehive, full of stray and seemingly uncon- nected ideas that slammed about his cranium, fight- ing for attention:

Where do all the words on the blackboard go when you erase them?

Torture is evil, but does it work?

Could Siara like me?

What would happen if all the oxygen molecules sud- denly drifted away and left us to suffocate?

Not all his thoughts were unconnected. Some flowed easily from one to the next, like, *Should I tell the nice security guards that the air might vanish? Should I warn them not to take air for granted?* Some were even quite reasonable, like, *Yeah, that'll go over big. I'm going to have enough trouble trying to explain the whole thing with the chairs.*

Of course, he'd have been happy to explain why he'd piled a bunch of chairs at the front of the auditorium, then refused to let them be touched. He'd have been thrilled with an opportunity to spell it all out, at length and in writing. Only there was one problem.

He had no idea.

It had seemed like a good idea *while* he was doing it. It had seemed like a great idea, life or death, but ever since he'd placed that final banana peel, all his perfect, subtle, cosmic reasons had vanished like a soupy dream. And all these crazy, fractured thoughts rushed in to fill the vacuum.

Is that a fake tie he's wearing?

What if you're meant to save him?

Did I leave the light on by the mattress?

Now he was in immediate danger of being shipped back to Windfree. Aside from hating every minute there, he didn't *deserve* to be sent there. He wasn't crazy. These crazy thoughts were just his broken-down filters. If anything, he was more in touch with what was going on in and around him. Just like he'd tried to explain to Siara.

Of course, there is this weird thing with the chairs. . . .

As they turned a corner, sunlight rushed in from the end of the corridor. Harry winced as it lit his face. It reminded him of Windfree. The whole hall did. Same barred window, same filthy tan halls, same thick, coffee-brown, coffin-like doors. And here he was, freaking out, being led along by two impatient guards who were acting like they might catch the crazies just by holding his arms. Seemed like old times.

Maybe it was all the same. Maybe it was all one prison or another.

No good deed goes unpunished, Mr. Keller!

A sharp firecracker snap from the auditorium made him jump, but he had no idea what the sound was. Didi and Gogo didn't react, so he figured it couldn't be all that important.

Gruff laughter from some passersby shook him. It had to be meant for him. Shame tingled over his body like a stinging rash. He zeroed in on the floor, hoping to make it go away.

You're a genius if you fly a kite during a thunderstorm and discover lightning is electricity—but you're an idiot if you fly a kite during a thunderstorm and discover lightning can kill you.

It seemed to work. Outer sounds muffled. The flakes of gold and silver breaking up the gray in the linoleum floor tiles filled his mind. Each seemed more and more unique until, in his mind, they glowed.

Well, hello, flakes! I guess it takes one to know one.

Only then, things went too far. The flakes started to rise, lifting from the linoleum expanse like stars in a light gray sky. They hovered *above* the scratches, mixing with one another, changing colors, shining, fading, shifting.

This can't be good.

The flakes twisted, ready to form pictures, whisper secrets in his ears. It felt like they were going to pull him down into the tiles, so far he'd never get back.

Come and be a tile with us! Linoleum is always happy!

That did it. His stomach twisted into knots. He couldn't pretend to be calm, or in control, or anything any longer. He tried curling himself into a protective ball, but Didi and Gogo only pulled him along harder and faster.

As they reached the door to the office of his guidance counselor, Mr. Tippicks, Harry heard sirens. Was it an ambulance? For him?

At practically the same moment, Didi's walkie-talkie squawked to life and he got a now-what? look on his face. He turned his back and spoke into it. Harry needed to be alone. Wrapping his arms around his gut and bending forward slightly, he just went inside the office. Neither guard tried to stop him.

The tiny office was empty. At least it was quieter here than in the hall, and the paper piles on the floor obscured his view of the wicked linoleum shards. Through the glass window in the top half of the door, Harry glimpsed Didi racing off, leaving Gogo behind. He slumped into a cheap plastic chair that wobbled under his weight and looked around.

He'd spoken with Hippie Dippy Tippicks in special ed, but this was the first time he'd been inside the counselor's office. It was quite big, for a closet stuffed with books and plants. It had an acrid incense smell.

He suddenly thought of Siara. He couldn't help wishing he were back talking to her. Even though being around her made him nervous, that little conversation had felt like a quiet island, like in her poem.

Weird, he hadn't thought about her in ages before today. Things like girls and the rest of life had been swept away when his father died. But before that, he'd always hoped to see her at RAW. She was the first girl he'd ever wanted to actually ask out, but his father wouldn't let him date in middle school. They'd had a big fight about that one. As usual, Harry lost.

He'd even felt saner talking to her—then he remembered how not-normal it was, how her handwriting shifted on the page, morphing into words that weren't there.

Simple crystal wishes . . .

He wasn't going crazy. He wasn't. There must be an explanation. There was always an explanation. Yes, schizophrenia was an explanation, but not really the option he wanted to invest in emotionally.

It's not paranoia if they're really out to get you. . . .

Concentrate. . . . Hold on. . . . What else is in here?

Hanging plants, papers, moldy books, some stacked Harry-high. What was with the micro-size of this room? Were they punishing Tippicks? Sure, that made sense. Tippicks was always ranting against this war or that, against SUVs or corporate America in general. Last year, Harry had watched, amazed, as he spent a whole class talking one student out of joining the ROTC. It had been a scandal. The school had been about to fire Tippicks, but a huge number of students and parents protested. Instead they'd taken away his class and shoved him here, where his advice could be more easily dismissed.

Mr. Harry Keller. I've been dealing with Todd Penderwhistle. . . .

Harry managed a half smile. Tippicks was a fellow loon.

"Mr. Harry Keller," Tippicks said as he entered. He squeezed past Harry's knees, bending his balding head forward where it caught a bright sheen from the fluorescents. With a waddle and a thud, he reached the frayed chair behind his desk. As he leaned back, a few white chest hairs poked from the open collar of a faded paisley shirt. His expression was uniquely serious, especially compared to his usual freewheeling look. It felt like having the Cookie Monster suddenly become severe.

"I've been dealing with Todd Penderwhistle," he began, in an equally serious tone.

Didn't I hear that somewhere before?

"The police have things in hand for now. But you know all about that, right?"

Harry made a face. "Right? No. What?"

Tippicks made a face back. "What? What, indeed?"

He picked up a piece of paper, squinted at it, then gave up and put on a pair of mod reading glasses that hung from a chain around his neck. Harry recognized the pink color of a security report.

Tippick's index finger tapped the time stamp, then he looked at his watch and gave a little laugh. "After," he said. "It happened just *after* you left. Jeremy Gronson was hit by a flying chair."

Ohmigod, one of my chairs killed Gronson!

"Is . . . is Jeremy okay?"

Tippicks nodded. "Fine. If anything, that chair saved him."

Saved him?

"So what were you doing? Mr. Kaufmann said you were disturbed; 'whacking out' was his phrase. The police will ask. It'd be easier to start with me."

Harry stiffened. "The police? I was . . . I was just rearranging chairs."

"Okay. I'll bite. Why?" Tippicks asked.

Harry pretended not to hear. "Sorry?"

"Why? Why were you rearranging chairs?"

I guess it was to save Jeremy. I saved Jeremy Gronson's life! But how the hell do I explain that without you thinking I'm insane?

Harry's eyes slowly circled, searching for divine intervention among the books and plants. Should he mention his theory about brain filters? If anyone would understand it, free-thinking Tippicks might. The guy even had a lava lamp.

Love many, trust few, and always paddle your own canoe.

"I . . . I don't know," Harry said.

31

Tippicks brushed the stubble on his cheek with the backs of his fingers. "Okay, life is large. Things *don't* always make sense. Right?"

Aside from his current apparent lack of sanity, Harry Keller's biggest problem was not knowing when to keep his mouth shut. It was practically a Keller family tradition to say exactly the wrong thing at the wrong time—something his father had proved this summer, in spades. At this particular moment, Harry struggled with himself not to say, *Wrong. God does* not *play dice with the universe. Everything* does *make sense.*

Saying such a thing out loud could very well lead to a very complicated conversation about filters, the words in Siara's poem that moved by themselves, and the friendly floating bits of shiny metal in the linoleum. And all that could easily get Harry an express ticket back to Windfree. So, though dying to disagree, he bit his tongue and tried to smile and nod in an ain't-I-just-wacky? kind of way.

Tippicks regarded him cautiously. "Did Todd Penderwhistle sell you anything?"

"Sell?"

"Like ecstasy, Mr. Keller. Special K? Pot? Crack? You're sweating and pale."

Harry jerked back, offended. "I don't do drugs."

Tippicks gave him a disbelieving half smile. "Not *ever*?"

Harry slumped. "Okay, once in seventh grade I did

some Ritalin. It was on a bet, to see if I could do everyone's homework. And I drink coffee, if Starbucks is the new crack. But that's all."

"It can stay between us. I think most of them should be legal anyway. . . ."

"I don't do drugs," Harry reiterated. "My father would kill me!"

Tippicks furrowed his brow.

"*Would* have . . . he would've killed me," Harry corrected, shifting his gaze down to the tips of his sneakers. "Look, if I wanted something mind-altering, all I'd have to do is call my board-certified, state-appointed psychiatrist, Dr. Helen Shapiro. I could have Ritalin, Prozac, Xanax, Paxil, anything. I could even have it delivered. But I don't. I didn't like what I was on in Windfree, and I have no intention of taking anything."

My skull is quite colorful enough without drugs, thank you very much.

Tippicks bobbed his head. "I'd stay away from the coffee, too, Mr. Keller. But let's move on. Did you see the gun?"

Harry's eyes went wide. "Gun? Like, bang bang?"

If there's a gun hanging on the wall in the first act, it must fire in the last.

The firecracker snap. The siren. Didi racing off to answer a call. It had been a gunshot. In the auditorium? That made sense, in an eerie kind of way. It was like some part of Harry had expected it. His memory caught the edge of the reasoning behind what he'd done with the chairs, why he'd been so frantic. It had to do with saving Jeremy's life . . . from a gunshot?

It's not the bullet, it's the hole.

"Yes," said Tippicks. "Someone fired a gun. Luckily, no one was hurt."

"Todd Penderwhistle," Harry said softly.

Tippicks started to say something, but Harry couldn't see him anymore, or the office, or anything else that was right in front of him. For the first time in ages, Harry's thoughts collapsed into silence. His whole head was filled with one vision. What he saw was a dark alley, a narrow slice of space between deserted buildings, ringed with rotting fire escapes, colored in shades of blue and gray. He was high up, far from the rats and the trash on the black, wet floor below. He heard a sound: *skrtch skrtch skrtch*. Something soft scraping something hard.

A balloon twisted leisurely in a silent wind. It was pink, not a little kid's pink or a girl's pink. It was a deep kind of pink that glowed with darkness. A huge clown, a monster clown, was printed on it in gaudy reds and blues. Its eyes were mad, like a demon's, its teeth wide and yellow. Past it, just past it, Harry saw the long black lizard coat of Todd Penderwhistle flapping in the air as Todd plummeted into the alley, down, down, down.

"Mr. Keller?" Tippicks's voice pulled him back. "You

were saying something about Todd Penderwhistle?"

The buzz of Harry's head rushed back in.

Oh my God, what happened? What the hell was that? Did I fall asleep? Did I just have a schizophrenic episode?

"I didn't know he had a gun," Harry said, half thinking aloud.

Tippicks leaned back thoughtfully. The leafy tendrils of a hanging plant tickled the side of his face. He brushed them aside, stared at nothing a moment, then gave off a peculiar little grunt that sounded both defeated and amused.

"Mr. Keller, relax. I don't think you had anything to do with the gun. I'll tell the police that. As for the chairs, call me a wide-eyed New Ager, but I like to believe there are senses beyond the usual five. The night before President Kennedy's assassination, the White House was flooded with calls from everyday, average people who had a premonition something might happen to him and felt compelled to warn him. They were dismissed as cranks, my sister among them. Maybe you just had this sense in the back of your head that something was wrong. It's possible. But we have to keep in mind that depression and mental illness are also real, though perhaps linked. Do you know Salvador Dalí?"

Hello, Dalí, well, hello, Dalí! It's so nice to have you back where you belong. . . .

Harry shrugged. "Surrealist painter. *The Persistence of Memory?* Melting clocks, that sort of thing?"

"Yes, that sort of thing. He once said, 'The difference between me and a madman is that I am not mad.' And I'm sure you know about the thin line between genius and insanity."

Harry nodded. *I walk the line. . . .*

Tippicks rubbed his hands. "A school full of special, smart kids is bound to have a higher-than-average incidence of emotional . . . challenges. We had two suicides last year. Three drug-related deaths. Both statistics up from the year before. The only reason I kept Penderwhistle around this long was because I was worried he'd kill himself. Now he's somebody else's problem. Not you. You're still mine."

"I'm not suicidal," Harry muttered. *Just attached to a higher reality. Sort of. Maybe. Should I mention the dancing shards?*

"Didn't say you were." Tippicks fumbled for a file, found it, and held it toward Harry. "Things were going great in special ed. I was about to recommend you be placed back in a few regular classes."

Harry's heart stopped. It was as if he'd just said, "I was about to hand you Siara Warner as a girlfriend." Since the death of his father, getting back to normal classes was the only goal he had.

"You were?"

Tippicks made a sincerely apologetic face. "I can't now," he said softly. "Even if you were acting on a sixth sense, even if you thought you were helping—this looks pretty crazy. You know that. No good deed goes unpunished, eh?"

That sounds familiar.

For a second, Harry saw Tippicks as if he were young again, a full head of long, curly, flowing red hair. He was rolling a thick joint, sitting in a room plastered with black-light posters of Jimi Hendrix and women with arched backs and impossibly large breasts. Harry shook the disconcerting image out of his head. This time, unlike the alley, it fled.

"So, back to square one. And look, despite what I said about Kennedy and premonitions, if you have *any* warning signs, the kinds of feelings you've been told about over and over, don't assume you're on the road to a great discovery, like that fellow in *A Beautiful Mind.* Tell someone about it. Me, Dr. Shapiro, a friend. Anyone. Okay?"

"Okay," Harry said, lying.

Tippicks pointed straight up. "They're watching, Mr. Keller."

Harry thought for a second Tippicks meant God and his dead father. Then he realized they were directly below the administrative offices.

"I know," Harry said solemnly.

Tippicks crumpled the security report and shot it toward the wastebasket. It tipped the rim and tumbled in. "This is gone. A sprinkling for the May queen, if you're familiar with the music of Led Zeppelin. The police want to talk to you about Todd, but they've got a whole auditorium to go through first. Principal Pirsig is closing the school for the rest of the day. Good thing it's Friday. Go home, beat the rush. Watch it on TV. Come back Monday, bright-eyed and bushy-tailed, with no more folding-chair incidents. Okay?"

"Right. Okay. Thanks."

"And look, Mr. Keller, Harry—I'm a lover of the stranger things in life. If anything like this happens again, if you get any weird premonitions, tell me about it, would you? I'd love to hear. Maybe we could track it down together."

"I . . . okay."

Tippicks scribbled out a pass, handed it to Harry, then rose and made the awkward effort of walking him the two feet to the door. "I know it's not easy losing a parent. The only thing that ranks higher on the anxiety scale is losing a child. The world just isn't what it used to be for you. *You're* no longer who you used to be. It takes a long time. But you'll get there, Mr. Keller, don't worry."

I'm no longer who I used to be, Harry thought. That made sense.

He found himself liking Tippicks. Should he tell him more? Maybe, but now was not the time.

Anyplace but now, anytime but here.

Back in the hall, students and teachers milled at the doors, peering toward the auditorium. Harry could make out several police officers. As he approached on his way to the front door, he saw some older, tired men in suits questioning some kids. Harry figured they were detectives. They looked just like the ones on TV.

Siara was among them, acting frightened and upset. He wanted to catch her eye as he passed but decided he wouldn't be able to handle it if the police questioned him now. So, feeling cowardly, he slipped past the crime scene.

Or was it an *attempted* crime scene? Or an *averted* crime scene?

At the main entrance, the ceiling opened up to the building's full three-story height, revealing a huge tile mosaic of Great Thinkers: Aristotle, Kepler, Galileo, Einstein, Bohr, and others. They had all once been thought of as crazy. If any were born today, Harry figured they'd be medicated and probably never bother to think daring thoughts or make grand discoveries. For Newton it had been an apple. Maybe for him it was chairs, dark alleys, and clown balloons.

Harry glanced down at the money he'd pulled out of his pocket for the bus to count it. The back of a dollar caught his eyes. Through shades of green, the eye on the pyramid winked, while below it, in the triangle, he saw an alleyway and a dark, falling form. He shoved the bill in his pocket, briefly worried he'd hurt the blinking eye, then stumbled along, feeling dizzy, to the bus stop in front of the school.

Just let me get home, just please don't let anyone see me like this.

At once, Didi came out. "Why aren't you talking with the police?" he said.

Harry silently presented his pass. As Didi scanned it, the dizziness increased. The security guard's body wouldn't sit still. Worse, it started changing. In seconds, it aged: plump flesh drying and deflating into a desiccated corpse, a corpse that melted into bone, bones that warped to dust. The dust hung in the air, sparkling like the metallic shards in linoleum, then coalesced into a sort of floating fetus that matured, midair, into a baby, a toddler, a child, and a teen. Didi was like one of those old time-lapse films of a flowering plant, opening and closing, being born, living, dying.

This time there was more. Not just thoughts, which he still might think were his own, but voices. The voices of men, women, and children flooded Harry's brain:

Oh, mira! Bernardo is taking his first steps.

You never pay attention. Where is your mind?

I love you so much. It's okay I'm pregnant.

Don't worry, I'll do the right thing.

No, I don't drink that much.

Hold the end here while you inhale.

Maybe you can be a guard or do something for your family.

It's a quiet school, but we have trouble on occasion.

Careful, man, they do random drug testing.

TV not working again and it's so hard to sleep at night
with the air conditioner on high and the baby crying
all the time . . .

A Didi corpse handed back Harry's pass. Then a two-year-old Didi waddled back into the school.

Voices meant schizophrenia. Harry was just the right age for early onset.

"No, no, no!" he said out loud. He was terrified Didi had heard him, but the guard kept on waddling. Fearful someone else might hear him, he bit the inside of his lip so hard his mouth flushed with the salty taste of blood. The pain worked. The voices dimmed to background noise. Didi resumed his usual shape.

The bus arrived. He stumbled on, comforted by the familiar smell of exhaust.

An old woman, folded in an old green coat too heavy for the weather, sat across from him and smiled. As she looked away, the wrinkles on her face flattened and faded.

In for a penny, in for a pound. Damn!

He looked around. It wasn't just one person aging, dying, then being reborn; everyone was doing it, on the bus, in the street—it was spreading like a virus. His head flooded with so many whiny insect voices, screaming, shouting, fast, then slow, whispering the infinite, intimate details of every moment of their lives, he could barely make out any words:

happy job coffee today

want a way to say to play I
jittery Jenkins sexy Stan what does she think of me now
the check is in the mail
the music the rush the climb the fall
nothing to die for nothing at all

The world was bursting out of its skin, trying to speak to him, but his father had always warned him not to speak to strangers.

"Not good," Harry mumbled, closing his eyes. "Not good at all."

He pressed his hands against his ears as hard as he could, ready to crack his own head right open just to stop the rush. It was no use. Even the intimate darkness on the inside of his eyelids was deformed. Black against black, it rushed about, shifting helter-skelter like an amusement park ride that had torn free of its moorings, free even of gravity, and was heading off into space.

I go there when I'm laughing, I go there when I cry.

Then it stopped, as quickly as it came. Ride over. Everybody out. Please exit carefully from the front of your head. He pushed his hair out of his eyes and noticed how badly his hand was shaking. Maybe medication wasn't such a bad idea.

No, no, no!

On autopilot, he dragged himself out at the right stop. Panting, he took a few slow steps toward the thick iron door that led to Aunt Shirley's warehouse loft. He couldn't tell her any of this, even if a miracle occurred and she was home. His mother's sister had been nice enough to become his guardian after his dad died, to let him move in and everything. But with her away days at a time on acting jobs or casting calls, it was like living alone. She also had a low tolerance for things she didn't think she could handle—and Harry's problems were high on the list.

So it wasn't all that much of a home, but he was still relieved to see it.

That is, until he felt the ground move beneath him.

No one else seemed to notice, but the sidewalk was moving. Not just moving, undulating, waving in patterns that made the asphalt crack and tear. It was just like a movie he'd seen in physics of the Tacoma Narrows Bridge in 1940. Wind had created a resonant wave that made the steel and concrete flutter like a length of paper. The waves got bigger until the bridge collapsed. Only now it was the sidewalk, and there was no wind.

Animal fear gripped him. He ran, full out, into the old building, up the stain-covered stone-and-metal steps, toward the graffiti-covered loft door. He shoved the key in the lock, twisted, desperately pushed the door open and . . .

. . . stopped short, wishing he were blind.

The living room wasn't there. The loft wasn't there. Instead he wavered on the brink of an abyss. A huge drop opened in front of him, into the dark alley he'd seen Todd Penderwhistle fall into. The clown balloon was here too, gently twisting in the air, smiling right at him.

"Not good," Harry said to the clown.

It nodded.

Siara wrinkled her nose at the smell of body odor and cologne wafting off the fat detective. He wasn't writing down enough of what she said, so she cleared her throat and told him for the third time that Harry Keller had saved Jeremy Gronson using a bunch of folding chairs and that Todd Penderwhistle had threatened to kill Harry.

"Yeah," the detective said.

He was ignoring her. She was a stupid kid, weirded out by witnessing a shooting.

Maybe he's right.

"You've got his name?" she asked, testing him.

"Jeremy Gronson."

"No! The student I heard him threaten!"

"Weller. Larry Weller."

"No. Keller, with a *K*."

The detective nodded, making his chins wobble. "We'll get a statement. Sheesh. You kids make this Penderwhistle guy sound like Dr. Doom. One guy told us Penderwhistle lost two fingers wrestling a sewer alligator. And I thought this school was where all the smart-asses went. No offense. Look, don't worry, Penderwhistle isn't going to be threatening anybody anymore for a long, long time. Guy's an idiot. Pulls a gun in front of an auditorium full of witnesses. He trying to kill himself or what?"

He scribbled something down. "Anything else you think I should know? See any drugs? Other weapons?"

She wanted to mention the chairs again, but right now they sounded right up there with the alligator in the sewer.

At the same moment, she caught a glimpse of Dr. Doom himself, Todd Penderwhistle. He was being escorted by two police officers toward a squad car. He was taller than both, their authority more in their uniforms and guns than in their physical form.

When Siara didn't speak, the detective turned to see what she was looking at.

"Not so tough now, eh?" he said reassuringly.

But he was wrong. Todd did look tough. And as one officer released his grip to open the door, the legendary, fingerless alligator wrestler spun and slammed his head into the second officer's chest, sending him across the hood. Hands cuffed behind his back, Todd ran into traffic, where he was surrounded by honking horns and screeching brakes.

The police officers shouted, but Todd didn't slow down. They drew guns but didn't fire. Too much risk of hitting all the innocent bystanders, Siara figured. All the police inside, all the detectives doing the interviewing, raced off after Todd into the distant landscape of gray buildings and grayer sky, but as far as Siara or anyone else watching could tell, they didn't catch him.

4. Harry leapt backward, trying to put distance between himself and the huge drop that had appeared behind the door. His back hit plaster—hard. He threw himself at the stairs, fell down half a flight, raced down the rest, then scrambled for the outdoors.

How much wood would a woodchuck chuck if a woodchuck could chuck wood?

The stray thoughts were still with him, but the smell of garbage and rotting leaves steadied him. At least everything felt familiar, even if he didn't. Brenton was, after all, the same neighborhood he'd lived in with his father, even if he was in a different building now. Across the street, as always, the row of cheap, six-story, brick-faced apartment buildings blocked any decent view of sky or sun. Harry's side of the street was also the same as it ever was: paper warehouses built in the forties, barely converted before being rented as lofts.

Nothing had changed. Nothing except him.

You are what you eat.

Even Morty, the local street person, stood in his usual spot. His shopping bags full of oily rags, he thrust his usual piece of cardboard that said, simply, *$*, at whoever passed by. No one knew his name. Harry called him Morty because of the sound he made as he held out his sign: "Mmoooortttiiyeee." Maybe he was saying, "Money" or, "Good morning." No one would ever know.

Please, please, I don't want to wind up like him, Harry thought.

The only difference between myself and a madman is that I am not mad.

He felt his face. It was wet, hot, feverish. He hadn't noticed before, but he was swaying on his feet.

Find something to focus on.

Lizzie Feldon, a neighborhood kid, maybe eleven years old, was playing across the street. She looked the way Harry felt—hopelessly out of place. Her clothes had clearly been bought last fall. The shirtsleeves ended above her wrists; the skirt was threadbare. Her still-boyish body had been stretched long and lean by hormones.

Change is the only constant.

She tossed a small pink ball against the wall and caught it, over and over, while chanting something, some kids' rhyme. He couldn't make out the words exactly, but they sounded sort of like

Nostradamus from Paramus
Looks for futures far beyond us
How many does he see?
One, two, three, four, five

Her voice was high-pitched but forced, as if cling-ing to childhood. It was also irritated, as if angry at what time had done to her.

You and me both, Harry thought.

Someone tossed a few coins at his feet. Two rolled, clinking each other before flopping flat on the pave-ment. When a few passersby gave him pitying glances, it dawned on him:

They think I'm with Morty. . . .

Yep, the bag man had shifted a few paces nearer. Harry's nostrils flared at the smell. Morty smiled as if he'd found a brother to share this last shame, this final failure.

"Mmoooorttttiiyeee!" Morty said.

Why wouldn't they think I was with him? Harry thought. His clothes, never new, had been torn during his mad rush from the loft, his shirt was drenched with sweat, his hair flopping into his face. All he needed was his own sign. Maybe he could put some strange symbol on it, like π or ψ.

Tears welled in his eyes, but his brain would not sync up. It was like it was watching him from some-where far above, passing judgment, thinking things far away from what he felt.

Seventy-six cents. Hmph. You'd think they could've left more.

"Nostradamus from Paramus . . ."

Then things got weird in earnest again. Colors skittered across the walls of the buildings like bug swarms. The street changed texture from dirt to grass to concrete.

Got to get a grip. I can figure this out. I can. I will not let go! I will not give up!

Sounds slowed and warped. Shapes bent toward, then away from him. Across the wobbling street, Lizzie's rubber ball made slow pink trails in the air.

Never mind. I give up! I so give up! I surrender! Please, just make it stop. . . .

A bill fluttered to his feet, joining the coins.

A dollar, eh? That's more like it.

Amid the swirl, a plump old neighborhood woman loudly *tsk-tsk*ed Morty and Harry. A caricature of youth was painted in thick makeup over the gray prune of her face, which sat monstrously beneath a perfectly coiffed mass of white hair. She looked like a clown, a mad clown.

From the depths of her purse, like a magician pulling a rabbit from a hat, she produced a shiny quarter. She tossed it at him and Morty, like they were animals in a cage. It bounced off Harry's shirt, hit the ground, then rolled, wobbled, tilted, and fell.

Only it hadn't done any of that yet.

It was still in her hand, glinting in a bit of afternoon sun. But it was *also* in the air, not quite yet fallen. It hit his chest, but at the same time, it was on the ground. It rolled on the asphalt but was also already lying flat.

His eyes shot back and forth between her hand, his chest, and the ground. He could practically hear his brain creak, trying to make some sense of what it was seeing. The quarter, if you could still call it that, stretched out of her hand, to his chest, and down to the pavement in a long, silvery tube.

A convoluted roar turned his head. A cherry-red SUV turned the corner, only it hadn't yet—its rear wheels were motionless at a stop sign, but its body moved, curving right at the intersection. Its headlights were halfway down the next block. If the coin looked like a silver tube, this looked like a giant alien caterpillar. The sound it made—long, loud, and distorted—Harry realized, was its engine, passing by again and again and again.

It came back to him in a rush. He *had* saved Jeremy Gronson, and it was because he'd seen something like this. He'd known Todd was going to shoot Jeremy—he'd seen their futures roll out in trails like the quarter and the SUV. And the folding chairs—it was as if some part of him had known the exact combination needed to avert what was about to happen.

To make everything make sense, like Dad said . . .

He'd seen things like this at Windfree too but had

thought it was a dream or a side effect of the meds.

I'm not crazy!

Tink! The quarter dutifully rolled to the ground.

Vrooom! The SUV turned the corner.

"Nostradamus from Paramus." Lizzie tossed her ball.

The feeling passed. Even the stray thoughts quieted. He felt considerably calmer—not calm enough to operate heavy machinery, but calmer.

His eyes settled on Lizzie. He watched the way her hands moved when she reached to catch the ball. Each time, they headed not to where the ball was, but where she thought the ball *would* be. An image of the future must be in her head too—but nobody would have called her crazy.

"Nostradamus from Paramus . . ."

Jeez, Harry thought. *Doesn't she ever shut up?*

Predicting the future was something the human mind tackled constantly, just to get from one place to another. Even crossing the street, you didn't react to where the cars were, but where you thought they *would* be.

So, (a) I'm not crazy, and (b) maybe what my brain is doing isn't so unusual after all. . . .

"Nostradamus from Paraaaaaaaaaaaaaaaaaaaaaaaaaaa . . ."

"You're *so* not the type to cut out like this, Warner," Debbie Hutchinson said, eyeing Siara with extreme disapproval. "I mean, the police asked you to stay until you signed your statement."

Hutch, a shorter girl with pale skin and smooth dark hair, held the emergency door open for Siara, first making sure a well-placed screwdriver had indeed temporarily disabled the alarm.

The look of disapproval melted into a wicked grin. "I'm so proud of you. IM me as soon as you can and let me know what this is all about. I'll check my cell every half hour. Delayed gratification is *so* not me."

Siara scrunched her face. "Um . . . computer's down. How about I just call via my landline?"

"How retro. Okay," Hutch answered. She glanced down the hall. "Didi and Gogo will be back any minute. Go for it."

Siara inwardly kicked herself as she raced out. She hated lying to Hutch, but she hadn't fessed up yet that the Warners were a one-computer family. Worse, it was five years old and sat in their living room, where Dad watched TV and Mom read. She didn't feel comfortable typing personal data there. Oh, most likely Hutch couldn't care less, but Siara didn't want to deal. There were more pressing matters at hand, like bad craziness and possible murder.

Todd Penderwhistle had threatened to kill Harry Keller, and now Todd was free. Maybe it *was* nothing, but Siara couldn't get Harry out of her mind—from her chat with him about "the consequences of time" right on up to the weird chair sculpture that, though she couldn't believe it, seemed to save Jeremy's life. After they hadn't spoken for years, he'd gotten himself stuck in her thoughts.

She worried he was depressed. She worried she'd been mean to him over her stupid poem. She worried he was feeling scared and lonely. Something about him had brought out the caretaker in her, an instinct that had ruled her last two relationships and that always left her with the short end of the stick.

But Harry was different—really hurting, really in need—and she certainly wasn't thinking about him in that way anymore. Was she?

No. She just wanted to warn him and make sure he was okay.

It shouldn't be too hard to figure out where he lived. She'd overheard Didi tell Gogo he'd been sent home, and Siara knew Harry and his aunt lived near Lydig. That was a short ride on the 28 bus. She could ask around once she got there.

Besides, how many Kellers could there be in a city of five million?

Am I being crazy? she wondered, but she shook her head, pushing the thought away.

She slipped into the crowd at the bus stop and looked for a familiar face. She'd have to borrow a cell to call home. Her parents had probably heard about the shooting already. She'd leave a message saying she was fine, checking on an upset friend. There'd be hell to pay if her parents found out she was bending the truth, but there would be plenty of time to worry about that later.

Right now, she was just trying to enjoy one of those beautiful September days when you really couldn't figure out how to dress. Her corduroy jacket and white sweater worked nicely in the brisk air, even matching the brown book bag that dangled from her shoulders. And actually, she looked pretty cute.

Oh God, please tell me I'm not worried about how I'll look for Harry Keller, she thought, just as the bus arrived.

No matter where you go, there you are.

Harry felt lifted, yanked hard in a direction he was unable to identify. Up, down, in, out? None of that made sense anymore. He felt like he had hands and feet, yet at the same time had the overwhelming feeling his body was being left far, far behind.

The good news was that the tumult inside his brain was gone.

The bad news was that it had decided to move outside.

Anything recognizable as the world was gone. Everything everywhere had turned into a trail, just like the SUV and the quarter. There were no single objects anymore, just one big mass, divided into three-dimensional paths of different textures that twisted, slid, intersected, and rose and fell from horizon to horizon. They formed plains, valleys, mountains—an entire new reality.

The stray thoughts, the sounds in Harry's head,

were outside him now—only faster, higher, gentler on the ear. He looked up, trying to place the source.

Above the tangled terrain was something like a sky, but its color kept changing, as if the red, blues, golds, greens, and yellows were just passing through, carried by the wind. There were no clouds, but among the wafting hues were definite shapes. They moved like living things: square mandala patterns, psychedelic butterflies that flapped from the center like wings. No, not flapped. Their lazy movements were more like those of the long flat fins of a stingray undulating through ocean water.

That was where the sounds were coming from! The flying creatures made an insect sound, not a voice, as Harry had heard before, but a continuous chime. Each one a little different, but all mixed together in a seamless harmony.

In spite of all the strangeness, he wanted to smile.

Is this heaven? Have I made that wild breakthrough Mr. Tippicks thought I could mistake for insanity? Has my brain actually done something useful, something wonderful *for a change?*

A heavier, grating sound brought his attention back down to the ground. The trail-filled terrain wasn't uninhabited, either. At first he thought some trails were just wobbling, but on closer inspection he spotted long, spindly appendages, like legs or arms, lifting a big round body, like that of a spider. It looked like it was made of the same stuff as the terrain. Maybe it was natural camouflage, the way a chameleon could change its color to match a rock it sat on? In any case, Harry could make out a few of these spider creatures not far off, rolling and poking about the furrows as if searching for food.

The world always makes sense. Sometimes we just fail to understand it.

It was half his father's voice, half his own, but enough to convince him that if he wasn't truly, absolutely, totally nuts, he was terribly lucky to be here. This was his Galileo moment, seeing that the earth was not the center of the universe. He should do his best to make sense of it. He stepped forward, feeling like an explorer who'd just landed on an unknown planet, fearful, but duty-bound to investigate.

That's one small step for man, one giant leap for a crazy person.

Whatever. At least it wasn't a stray thought, at least it was him, trying to tell a lousy joke. Most of this weird place was trails, so they were a likely place to start. He looked around to choose one for a closer look.

One seemed to stand out. It looked softer, gentler than the others. Looking at it made him tingle. He tried to walk over and soon found himself bouncing along on the springy surfaces of the trails, until he reached his destination and knelt on top of it.

It didn't look any different close up than it did from far away—kind of globby, like a solid stream, if that made sense, or one of those movie robots that could change shape and ooze into small places. He put his hands down to touch the surface. Though it was solid beneath his feet, with just a little pressure from his fingertips, his hands disappeared up to the wrist, passing into the trail. His unseen hands quivered. It felt like he was holding wet clay, only clay that refused to actually touch him but surrounded his hands and put pressure on them just the same.

Cool!

He pulled his hands out to make sure they were still there, then pressed them back down, harder this time. The stuff tingled around his fingertips—and abruptly gave.

Whoops!

Up to his elbows in trail, he couldn't stop himself from falling forward. First his head, then his torso tumbled. Before he knew it, he was inside.

Inside *what*?

Kind of a tunnel, but not quite. It had direction, left and right, but it wasn't exactly hollow. Disorienting images rose around him, forming recognizable shapes and sounds. Books, faces, kids from school, then someone being interviewed by a police detective.

Siara.

It was Siara, standing in a hallway at RAW.

"Hey! Siara! Hey!" Harry said. He felt like he was just a few feet from her. He waved, but she didn't see him. It was like she, the detective, and everyone else in

57

the hallway were ghosts, acting out their lives, oblivious to his existence.

Or is it the other way around? Am I the ghost?

He looked at his hands. Five fingers. He looked at himself—legs, torso, even clothes. How could *he* be the same shape if nothing else was? Maybe this wasn't his body exactly, just some kind of a projection. So maybe the trails and everything else were solid and *he* wasn't. Made sense, sort of. If you accepted a loose definition of the word *sense*.

He moved along, slowly at first. Images continued to leap in and out of the watery oneness. The detective interviewing Siara made him feel uncomfortable, like he wasn't listening. Then he realized it was *Siara's* discomfort he was feeling. He felt her tense and stare as she watched Todd escape from the police.

It dawned on him—*I'm in Siara's life! This trail is Siara!*

He pushed ahead one way on the still-soft ground and saw her get on a bus.

Is this her future?

He ran in the other direction. All at once the ground became hard, like cement. He saw her rise from bed that morning.

Is this her past? Is the past hard, like, set in stone?

He watched her head into the bathroom, turn on the shower, and start to remove her terry-cloth robe. He stared at her soft shoulders, marveled at the way her skin hugged her collarbone, and . . .

Whoa.

Embarrassed, he pulled at the side of the trail and stumbled forward, then kicked himself for being such a prude.

Jeez, Dad, thanks for the ethics and everything, but couldn't we have been, like, a little more pagan? I mean, no one would ever have known. . . .

Looking up, he saw the RAW study hall. Siara was sitting, working on the poem she'd shown him, trying to use some sort of clock imagery. Siara was fully clothed here, so he was able to pay more attention to everything else—the auditorium chairs, the high walls, even the clock. He found the clock annoying and knew he was feeling her think:

Probably feels trapped. It must feel trapped. Maybe it's dying to stop circling, to crack the plastic cover, zip out all over the place and make wild zigzag patterns on the walls. Then no one will ever get to class again.

There was more. Not just the clock. There was something different about everything, like they weren't just things, like they were somehow alive, related, all to each other and all to Siara.

Another revelation dawned. He wasn't just hearing her think; he was sensing the entire world from her point of view—the colors that pleased her, the smells that wrinkled her nose, the textures that graced her skin—everything seemed to speak, only it wasn't her thoughts exactly, more like a narrator in a book:

No use. The clock was non-poetic, if that was a word. Maybe it was a-poetic, like amoral, asymmetric, or a-pain-in-the-ass. Tick. Tick. Tick.

Was this like the brain filter he was talking about? A voice in everyone's brain that wove their senses into a story so they'd know what to pay attention to and what to ignore? Here in this trail, he could hear it as if it were his own:

She blew a puff of air to dislodge some plum-red hairs from in front of her right eye. She'd dyed a few strands last week, thinking it'd be a cool counterpoint to the rest of her long, dirt-brown hair, but now the hairs had a different texture, like half-dried papier-mâché. They were always flopping into her eyes, trying to blind her.

Ha! He was liking her even more—if that was possible—and her frustrated mental wrestling was giving him a cool idea: *A-Time*. That was exactly what this whole weird place he was in felt like. A-Time, as in bereft of linear time. Sounded better than Non-Time, anyway.

This also explained his stray thoughts. He'd been right—his own narrator, his own filter was broken somehow, maybe by the trauma of his father's death. It wasn't sure what to let in and what to keep out. Flashes from out of time had been breaking through to him.

Dad's death brought me here? But lots of people die. You'd think the place would be full of people. . . . Am I really that special?

As the moment when Harry had met Siara that morning approached, Harry felt an inexplicable, undeniable urge to leave. He clambered out, back into the open terrain, utterly uncertain why he'd left, disappointed that he had. The thought of seeing himself was as intriguing as it was frightening. What did he look like, really? Seeing himself in a mirror was one thing, but this would be much more au naturel.

And more important—what did he look like to Siara? What did she think of him? Was he just some basket case she felt sorry for, or did she get the same sort of ocean tingle Harry got from seeing her?

A new thought popped into his head: *If that was Siara's life, mine's here somewhere too.*

He'd left her trail at the moment they met, so his life must be somewhere around here. . . .

Ah! He saw it.

It looped briefly into Siara's. As he scanned its odd path back into the past and ahead into the future, he noticed it seemed to have lots more curves and dips than the relatively straight paths around it.

I always figured I was a little different.

So could he see his own future? Relive his past?

He raced over and dived inside. He caught a glimpse of himself standing next to Morty, but all of a sudden, all he could see was himself watching himself watching himself watching himself. The mirror images, rather than stopping or settling down, doubled and doubled, faster and faster, until finally, with an explosive *poit!*—Harry was unceremoniously ejected from his life trail, headfirst.

He flew into the air a few feet, then tumbled to the ground.

What the hell was that about?

His body was relatively unhurt, so he straightened his clothes and stepped up to try again. Tentatively he pressed his foot back into his life trail. It wobbled, as if an electric current were passing through it. As the discomfort increased, he pulled it out again.

I guess that's not allowed, he mused, again disappointed. *Was that why I had to leave Siara's trail before I came on the scene?*

Skrunk!

A sound made him spin around. One of those bulbous spider monsters was poking around a particularly dark and foreboding trail. This monster was bigger than the others, a head or so taller than he was, and thick, like an elephant. It was uglier than the others too, if that were possible. And if Siara's trail was welcoming, the one this thing poked around had *Keep the freak away!* written all over it.

Hoping the creature wouldn't notice, Harry tried to get closer. Its body was nearly all mouth—surrounded by rows of sharp, sharp teeth.

The better to eat you with, my dear!

Worse, in its center, at the end of a tongue-like stalk

as thick as Harry's leg, was a single, huge, horrible eye.

Seeing it, Harry gasped loudly.

When he did, the stalk twisted in his direction.

The eye looked right at him and blinked, its lid spreading a thin coat of mucus over the eyeball.

If that wasn't enough to make Harry totally freak, at the same moment, the image of the alley crashed into his mind. He'd hoped his head would be free of visions now that he was in this strange world, but this one arrived with the same tactile force he'd experienced inside Siara's trail.

Instead of the shimmering, living world of a would-be poet he had a thing for, now he felt utter despair—a hopeless nothingness, loneliness like the cosmos must have felt before there was life, and a deep enveloping desire not to feel anything anymore. Then he saw Todd Penderwhistle plummet into the alley to his death. Only he knew Todd wasn't frightened by it: he wanted it, he wanted it badly—and Harry, sensing it now from Todd's point of view, wanted it too. *This is Todd's life,* Harry realized.

The balloon twisted around and the clown laughed.

Todd's going to jump out of a window. He's going to kill himself. Soon. And it has something to do with the monster sniffing at his trail. But what?

The image fled, leaving Harry to stumble away from the gaze of that horrible eye.

No longer feeling like a fortunate Columbus on the shore of the New World, he dived for cover behind a swelling in the trails and stayed there until he was confident the thing wasn't looking at him anymore.

"Veni, vidi, volo in domom rediere," Harry whispered to no one in particular.

It was Latin, a language his father had started teaching him when he was nine. Harry was fond of making up his own Latin sayings. Roughly translated, this one meant: "I came, I saw, I want to go home now."

5. "Wake up! Wake up! Oh, God! Are you dead? Don't be dead!!"

Harry's head didn't quite feel like his head. It bobbed as if it belonged more on a little toy dog in the back of a car. Someone shook his shoulders, though they didn't feel exactly like his shoulders, either. His ears *did* feel like his ears, and when someone again screamed, "Harry! Wake up!"—it gave him a headache.

He opened his eyes. It was Siara. Shrill, screeching, but Siara. Was this a dream? She seemed upset.

And what about him? Where was he? He was on the ground, sitting in something wet, afraid to think what.

"Harry!"

"Shhh!" he said, wincing. "I'm not deaf!"

He heard her exhale. "Not deaf? I thought you were dead! You were all white! I couldn't tell if you were breathing! It was like you were in a coma!"

"Oh yeah," he said. "That."

"Yeah, that!" she said. She punched him hard on the shoulder.

"Ow!" Harry said.

"Are you okay?"

"Sure, it was just my shoulder, and you hit like a girl. . . ."

"That was for scaring the crap out of me! I meant

are you okay about the coma and the not breathing!?"

"Yeah. I think I'm fine." He looked at her again, suddenly realizing it was odd for her to be here at all. "Siara. How'd you get here?"

"I took a bus," she answered.

He scanned his surroundings, snapping his head back and forth, surprised by everything. The trails were gone. The creatures were gone. The sky was a normal color.

"So you didn't get to me *there*. I got back to you *here*," he said.

"What are you talking about? Listen, Todd escaped from the police. . . ."

"I know."

"You *know*?"

"Yeah," he said. "I saw it. He got away from the two cops. Don't worry. I think Todd's going to kill himself tonight."

He touched the brick wall and smiled slightly, really, really happy it was there.

"Don't worry?" she said.

He nodded toward her hands, which were again gripping his shoulders tightly. "Do you mind if I, um . . . get up? Alley floor's kinda damp . . ."

She pulled back. Harry couldn't tell if she was surprised or annoyed.

"You know about Todd. How do you know? Was it on the news?" she said.

Satisfied his pants weren't soaked, Harry rubbed his face and talked into his hands. "How do I know? Well, that's just a teeny-tiny bit hard to explain."

"Try me," Siara said.

He stuck his hand out and helped her pull herself to her feet. She tugged her jacket around her tightly. The wind, stronger now, was funneled down the alley by the buildings.

"If it's going to be a long speech like your brain-filters thing, could we please go inside somewhere before you start?"

"No, it's okay. I'm fine, really."

"Good for you, but *I'm* cold. I'd like to go inside. Do you live near here, like somewhere where there's an actual adult present in case you go comatose again?"

Harry looked across the street. The sky was still blue, but the sun had dipped below the building tops, leaving everything in a cool shadow. How long had he been gone? How long would he be staying? He'd have to tell Siara something fast; otherwise, if he looked like he was in a coma again, she'd probably call an ambulance. Then he'd wake up at Windfree for sure.

"My aunt's loft is around the corner," he said. Against his natural instinct to avoid such contact, he looked Siara in the eyes. *Should I trust you?*

"There's something I have to tell you," he said. "Something . . . complicated, something you'll have a hard time believing."

She was taken aback. He figured it was his gaze. She was used to seeing his eyes bounce all over the place, but ever since she woke him, he was feeling unusually focused.

"Could you give me the short version before I get frostbite?"

"Okay. I was right. I'm not crazy," he said. "I've just accessed a state of consciousness where I can perceive reality without the benefit of linear time."

Siara's eyes got wider. Her upper lip curled. "Oh. Right. Um, is your aunt home?"

He smiled. "That doesn't sound so good, does it?"

He motioned toward the sidewalk, indicating that she should go first. She didn't move until a blast of cold air convinced her, and they were soon walking side by side.

He held the door to his building open for her.

"You came all this way just to warn me about Todd?" Harry said, unable to conceal the fact that he was pleased.

She scowled as she stepped in. "It wasn't all that far. Someone had to. Todd said he wanted to kill you."

"Thanks," he said, following her inside.

Feeling embarrassed by the place, Harry watched her look around. Old cast-iron radiators hissed and clanked as if accomplishing something, but the hallway was no warmer than outside. The white stone stairs were cracked, the iron railings rendered thick and ungainly from a million coats of cheap black paint. The whole place smelled of something awful cooking. *Cabbage?*

"It's home," Harry said.

They trotted up the two flights. He paused at the large, steel, graffiti-covered door. A single word, painted in red spray paint, stood out from the rest.

"Squalor?" Siara said.

He shrugged. "Been there months. Makes sense, I guess, given the surroundings. Not a bad word, really. Squalor is chaos, and chaos is how the world began. It's a very creative word when you think about it."

"Okay, 'Squalor,' open the door already," she said, rubbing her hands together.

Half expecting the staggering drop he'd seen the last time he opened the door, Harry braced himself, then pushed. They were greeted by familiar exposed-brick walls, an old green couch with a few tears in the fabric, scattered books and magazines, an old turntable, and some huge windows.

Harry must have looked surprised, because Siara asked, "This *is* your apartment, right?"

"It is this time," he said, stepping in.

"Where's your aunt?" She walked in and looked around.

"She's not here much. Acting. I'm sort of on my own. Child welfare checks up on me once a week," Harry said, wincing. "I wish at least they'd call it 'teen' welfare or something. It feels kind of stupid."

"I can't imagine being alone that much. My parents are always around," she said. She seemed nervous. He could tell she was disappointed his aunt was gone.

"Don't worry," he said. "I don't bite or anything."

She flashed a little smile. "It's not that. I just really think we should get you to a doctor. Is there someone you can call?"

He shook his head, held out his steady hands. "No, no. Look. I'm fine. Not shaking, not sweating anymore . . ."

"You were sweating?" Siara said. "You could be having seizures." In a blink, she breached the unspoken no-touch code and put her hand on his forehead.

He liked the way it felt. "See? Fine."

But it wasn't fine. He watched as she spotted exactly what he'd hoped she wouldn't—the list of emergency numbers his aunt had written, posted on the wall near a small black cordless phone, with *Doctor* topping the list. Reaching for the phone, she announced, "You're going to a doctor."

Violating the no-touch rule himself, he gently grabbed her hand. "No, wait, please. Send me to a hospital and I'll end up trying to explain all this to some intern and they'll just lock me up again. You came here to help me, right? Lemme just . . . lemme just *try* to make you understand. Please?"

"You want me to understand about accessing a state of consciousness where you can perceive reality without linear time?" Siara asked.

"Well, yeah," he said hopefully.

She started dialing.

"Wait, wait, wait!" Harry said.

She kept dialing.

"No! Look, how can I— The auditorium! Those chairs saved Jeremy Gronson, didn't they? A chair hit him in the gut and the bullet missed his head, didn't it?" Harry said.

She hesitated. "So?"

"So how did I know? I just described it to you, and I wasn't even there! Well, okay, Mr. Tippicks told me about it. But how did I know to set up the chairs in the first place? Doesn't that prove I'm not crazy?" he asked excitedly.

"No," Siara answered. "It proves that maybe you're not *just* crazy."

But with one number to go, she stopped dialing.

"Look, here's some honesty. Deal with it. I'm a little scared for you, and I'm a little scared *of* you . . ." she said.

Harry nearly laughed. "Really? I'm so totally harmless," he said. He tried to make his pleading face look as pathetic as possible. Apparently it worked, because she put down the phone.

"Okay. Five minutes."

Harry clapped. "Okay. Nature of reality in five minutes. No problem. Um . . . remember what I said about all the data that hits you, and the brain filters that sort them out?"

"Kind of. Is this a quiz?"

"No, but there'll be a test after class. Now stay with me, please. Suppose I'm right about the filters. Now suppose that time—you know, linear time, tick, tick, tick, hour after hour, that sort of thing—isn't really real. Suppose it's more like a map; suppose it's one of those brain filters?"

She scrunched her face. "How can time not be real? If time's not real, nothing's real."

"Good question," he said, pointing at her. "Extra points for Siara Warner. How can time not be real? Well . . ."

Frustrated, he started making faces. Her hand moved toward the phone again.

"Stop! Okay! Got it! You know the big bang theory from science, right? In the beginning, everything everywhere in the universe was really just one big thing until it blew into pieces? Well, maybe it didn't blow into pieces at all. Maybe the universe isn't a bunch of little things; maybe it's still one big thing. So maybe time isn't really made up of separate events, the way we think; maybe it's just one big event. Whaddaya think, huh?"

"I think I don't understand a word you just said," Siara said, slumping into a chair. "I also think I have a headache and would like some coffee."

"That's a good example, you and your headache—you talk about them like they're separate things, but are they really? Aren't they really part of the same thing?"

"Yes, they are," she answered slowly. "And both my headache and I would also like to become one with a cup of coffee."

He laughed nervously. "Coffee, yes. I'll make coffee. You know, I like to drink it myself."

"I can tell."

He rummaged about the nook that contained fridge, sink, stove, and cabinets. Feeling watched, he pulled a can from the freezer and a filter from the cabinet.

What does a crazy person look like? he wondered. *What should I not be doing?*

"Do you get what I'm saying so far, sort of?" he said.

He searched her face for any sign of understanding. She gave none.

"*Sort of* is the operative word," Siara answered.

"Um . . . that's two words. But never mind, that's okay. How about . . . how about the blind men and the elephant?" He found a scoop and shuffled ground beans into the filter.

"Who's the blind man, me or my headache?" Siara said.

"The blind *men* and the elephant. Check it out: Three blind men are brought before an elephant for the first time, and they try to figure out what it is. One feels the big, flat side of the elephant and says, Hey, an elephant's like a wall. One feels the tail and says, No, an elephant is like a rope. The third feels the trunk and

73

says, No, an elephant is like a snake. They're all right; they're just not seeing the whole picture. Maybe it's like that with time. Everyone's filters blind them to the whole picture, so all we see are the pieces, the rope, the wall, the snake. But it's possible to see more. And that's what's happening to me. I'm seeing more." By the time he was done, he'd spooned seven scoops into the overburdened filter. "Crazy, huh?"

She rose, stepped next to him, and took the scoop from his hand. "Okay, um . . . so the elephant is the world, and we're all blind except you?"

"That's it! Exactly!" he said happily.

"What did your shrink say again about you being narcissistic and delusional?"

His face fell. "I'm not doing this for fun, you know."

"I know," she admitted. "The thing with the chairs weirded me out. And the thing that really scares me now is that I . . . I think something really is going on with you."

"You do?" Harry said. Impulsively he grabbed her and hugged her.

She stayed close for a moment, not pulling back, and then Harry realized what he was doing and dropped his arms back to his sides.

"Sorry, sorry," he said, turning quickly back to the coffee.

Siara ran her hand through her hair and cleared her

throat. "So, back in the alley you were, like, in your higher state of consciousness?"

Pouring water into the coffee machine, he said, "Exactly, only it feels like traveling to a whole other place, where past, present, and future coexist. It's like . . ." He paused, remembering Siara's thoughts about the clock when he'd been in her life trail and the name it had helped him come up with. "Well, it's sort of like A-Time. You know, like amoral or asymmetric."

She raised an eyebrow. "You're naming your hallucinations now?"

"Well, it's not like I called it Me-Time," he said. He flipped the coffee machine on.

"It's cool. I had an imaginary friend named Mr. Truffles. Of course, I was six," she said.

"I wish I could show it to you." he said. "It'd make this so much easier."

"How did you get there?" she asked. "What does it feel like?"

Harry shook his head and paced. "Dunno. Maybe when my father died, I became so numb to all the things I used to care about that my brain started letting other things through."

"But then everyone who had a relative who died would get to A-Time."

"Yeah, you'd think. Maybe mediums get a glimpse of it, and that's how they see the future. Maybe I had a predisposition. I am . . . you know. . . ." He waved his hands and nodded at her, as if the answer were obvious.

"Self-conscious? Paranoid?" she offered.

"No. Um . . . really smart."

Again she raised a single eyebrow. Harry had always wished he could do that.

"Humble, too," she said. "What kind of things does your brain pay attention to?"

Harry shrugged. "I'll just focus on something, patterns on the floor, someone's face, a quarter, a ball. Maybe it can be anything." He pointed to a gangly thing in a pot near the window that desperately needed water. "Like that plant. You know how if you say a word over and over it sort of stops sounding like a word? Same with the plant. It's like the edges aren't really edges, like it's really part of the air and the dirt and the room. If I stare long enough, those edges start to vanish. . . ."

He wavered on his feet.

"Harry?" Siara said.

The leaves changed from brown to green. A bud flowered and fell. The stem withdrew into a buried seed.

"You okay? Your eyes are getting all fuzzy."

A seedling shot out from the dirt. The slender stalk thickened and changed from green to thick brown. Branches curled out like arms; the brown stem thickened into a back. One minute it was a plant, the next it was a coat, flapping in the wind. Todd, plummeting, falling, down, down, down. A pink balloon floated nearby, slowly turning. . . .

"*Harry!*"

A hand poked him on the shoulder. He jumped, surprised Siara was so close. Sweat beaded on his forehead. She touched his face but pulled back immediately and raced for the phone.

"*No!*" Harry screamed. His voice was so loud she shivered. Instead of the phone, she started eyeing the door.

Oh, crap . . .

"Thought you said you were harmless," she said.

He lowered his voice. "It's Todd. I keep getting this vision. He's jumping out a window, off a building. Like I said, he's going to kill himself. Tonight. I just don't know where, but I keep seeing it, over and over. At first I thought it was just wishful thinking."

He forced a smile. "That last part was a joke. I *am* harmless, I swear."

Siara shook her head. "I don't think you are, Harry Keller. I don't think you're nearly as harmless as you think."

He kind of liked the sound of that. But her hand was still on the phone.

"Look," she pleaded. "Let me call my mother. She works in a physics lab. She's just an assistant, but maybe she'll know a time specialist or something. . . ."

"No," Harry whispered, shaking his head.

He walked up to her slowly and gently took the phone from her hand. They were standing close, very close. Siara started to shake and when Harry reached out to hug her, her eyes got watery.

She's really worried about me. Wow.

"You are so annoying. I just don't know what to do here," she said.

"Me neither," he admitted. Without realizing it, he pulled her closer and caught a whiff of fruity shampoo in her hair. His heart beat faster, and this time he didn't let go of her so quickly. He wasn't usually this close to a girl, especially not one like Siara. He closed his eyes, hoping to forget all the craziness for a second, to enjoy the moment, but no such luck.

A rush of black against black filled his head. Instead of beating pleasantly with excitement, his heart began to hammer with dread. He felt himself going, going back to that strange place, back to A-Time. If he did, and he went into that coma thing, she'd call a doctor. He'd go back to Windfree. He fought the spinning inside him back down.

Siara didn't seem to want to leave the embrace, but he pushed her slowly away, saying again and again, "I'm okay. I'm okay. Really, I'm okay." She looked at him and shook her head.

"Are you stoned?"

"No! Why does everyone think I'm on drugs? Look, there must be a way for me to show you, to make you see what I see. I can describe it. Talk you through it. But you have to be open. You have to let the way you look at the world really change. You have to stop believing in things and start seeing systems. . . ."

How do I do this?

He snapped his fingers, then pulled her into the center of the room and practically pushed her down onto the mattress he used as a bed. "Get comfortable. I want to try something."

She raised that eyebrow again but did what he asked. He rushed over to the ancient turntable, swatted away a few of his CDs, and put on one of his aunt's old Beatles LPs. The song filled the air, somehow making everything feel even more bizarre.

"Hey, this sounds kind of familiar," Siara said. "Like something I've heard in the background, while my dad was watching VH1."

"Music is a system, one we're all used to paying attention to. Close your eyes and listen," Harry said. "Steady your breath. Relax."

"Kind of a nice psychedelic tune."

"Shhh. I said relax. It's kind of the opposite of what I'm talking about," Harry said. "First you hear it all at once; then, if you pay attention, you hear the pieces."

She started to talk again, but he raised a finger to his lips. "Shhh. Just listen."

6. Siara tried to relax and nestle into the sound of the old Beatles song playing, but it wasn't easy. She was worried about Harry, seriously wondering if he was a total nutcase, and *still* couldn't stop thinking about how close they'd just come to kissing. And how, despite everything else, she'd really, really wanted to kiss him.

Siara let out a deep breath, focusing completely on the music and pushing her thoughts away as much as possible. After a while, her breathing and her heartbeat moved in time. At first she heard it all at once, like Harry said, one sound, but after a while, she heard the parts each instrument played, the melodies. She heard how the pieces wove around one another, like the strands of a quilt. Then things started shifting: one second she heard the pieces, the next they all melted back into a single sound.

Is this what he meant? The parts and the elephant?

Just as she thought she was really getting the idea, the music stopped. He'd lifted the needle from the groove.

"Here's something you can't do with a CD," he said, and started spinning the black disc backward.

This time, she heard the pieces first, not the whole. They sounded off, bizarre, unsettling. Then portions started building, one on top of the other, like little rocks falling down the side of a hill, joining other little rocks and bigger rocks until finally they were causing an avalanche.

She felt the same terrifying rush she had in the auditorium right after Harry said *death*. Again she had the acute sense that something big and horrible was rising up right behind her. She felt like she was about to scream.

"Damn it!" Harry said impatiently, utterly unaware of her turmoil. He stopped. "This isn't going to work!"

She snapped open her eyes.

He walked over, knelt beside her, and put his hands on her shoulders. Her pulse started to race. A wild mixture of fear and familiar nervous jitters stirred inside her as she looked into his eyes.

His face close, he spoke in a low voice, and she could almost feel his breath on her skin. His eyes stayed focused on hers, and she remembered that look from middle school, the feeling that you had his total attention, as if you were the only person in the world.

"I need a way to make you feel like you're part of something larger, something infinitely big. You can't just *think* it; you have to *feel* it. How can I make you feel that?"

She shivered, feeling chills travel up and down her spine. God, she was feeling *something* right now. Something she'd never felt before, like there was an actual electric charge going back and forth between them. . . .

"How can I change your perspective? What can I do to make you feel something totally new, something to get past your filters, open your heart and your mind?"

His lips were inches from hers.

"How can I . . ." he began.

She leaned forward and pressed her lips against his, swallowing the second half of what he was about to say. She expected him to hesitate, like he did with everything else, but without a beat, his arms slid from her shoulders to her waist and pulled her closer.

He deepened the kiss. Siara let out a sigh as she reached her hands around his shoulders. A dizzying, swimming sensation took over her senses.

Then a thought came into her mind, from nowhere: *The second hand broke free of the clock, and the dish ran away with the spoon.*

She felt a tug, back and out, at the base of her skull, as if her spirit were being sucked through a small hole on the back of her neck. Her skin tingled, but was it from a gentle wind or was she underwater?

She opened her eyes. One minute she was being kissed, kissing, happily losing the line between her body and Harry's, then all of a sudden it was Charlie and the Chocolate Factory, Dorothy and Oz, Wendy and Neverland.

She imagined this was what a baby saw when it was born: first nothing, new eyes and ears blinded by sensation, then the part of it that sees and the part of it that wants work together for the very first time to sort out the world, putting this here, that there, until eventually God says, "Let there be light." And there is.

Or something like that.

This is crazy! Did I catch craziness from Harry? Just from kissing him?

That sounded like getting pregnant from a toilet seat, but all of a sudden it seemed anything was possible. It no longer felt like she was inside the loft or inside anything. Everything had spun into new and different shapes, reaching from horizon to horizon, and even these shapes wouldn't sit still. Horribly bright colors beamed around, vibrating, refusing to stay with things, as if colors were things themselves.

The only recognizable thing was Harry, and even he wasn't acting quite like Harry. For one thing, he seemed ridiculously happy. If this was from one kiss, what would happen to him if they ever . . . ?

"Welcome to A-Time!" he shouted.

He was jumping up and down on a funny little hill. The surface was springy, like a trampoline, and each jump sent him flying a little higher into the . . . the . . .

What the hell was that, anyway? It sure didn't look like the sky.

"I can't believe I brought you here!" Harry said.

What do you mean "you"? Siara thought, remembering she'd had something to do with it.

He bounded over. The ground wobbled beneath her when he landed. It felt like they were dreaming the same dream.

She looked at the face she'd just kissed. The weird smug smile aside, he actually looked different. All traces of extreme self-consciousness were gone. His hair wasn't covering his face anymore. She could see the clear skin of his forehead, the sharp, angular jawline. He looked . . . clean. Free of whatever it was that seemed to hang over him at school.

He waved at the indistinguishable mess around him. "I know it's kind of scary at first, but is this the best or what?"

The best what? she wanted to say. Instead she staggered a little and sat down. He came closer and put his hand on her head. It felt funny, not quite like his hand or her head.

His voice was a little worried, about her probably, but still cheerful. "Put your head bctween your knees. I don't know if we actually breathe here. I mean, I'm not sure we really have lungs or regular bodies, but it might help, psychologically, if you tried."

She closed her eyes, but it didn't help. He started massaging her neck.

(Was that her neck? Were those his fingers?)

"If there's no time, how can we see each other? How can we move?" she asked.

(Was that her tongue? Her teeth it clicked against?)

"I dunno," Harry said. "Maybe part of us is timeless?"

"It's like being high," she said wistfully. No sooner had she said it than she realized it might be true. "Did you slip something into the coffee?"

He seemed hurt. "No! I didn't slip you anything, I swear. I'd never do anything like that to anyone, let alone— Anyway, it's all one hundred percent natural, and real . . . and . . . healthy, and full of vitamins and minerals, and . . . and I didn't even really know any of that until someone else, I mean, until you came here. So . . . thanks."

Siara tingled and felt a little raw.

"You're welcome, I guess," was all she managed. "Only now I think we should *both* be locked up."

Harry fell silent. Afraid she'd hurt him, even more afraid he might move away and leave her alone in this weird place, she took hold of his hand.

"I didn't mean that," she said. "You have to admit this is pretty extreme."

He shrugged. "Yeah, but I did figure out a thing or two about it. I can show you . . . but . . ."

"What?"

"You'll have to open your eyes again."

"Really?"

"Yes."

"Okay. Fair enough."

As she did, her field of vision filled with Harry's face. It was awkward to have him so close, but much better than seeing all the weirdness that surrounded him. His hopeful expression looked so . . . funny it made her giggle.

"What?" he said.

She shrugged. "Go ahead, Professor."

He nodded. "Okay. Let's start with the simple stuff. The terrain we're on?" He pushed his hands down onto the springy surface. "These are trails, made up of the movements of things and people through time. Go on, touch it."

She didn't want to touch it or anything here, but he took her hands and gently brought them down. It was squishy, like a sponge, but the texture didn't make sense to her fingertips. It felt both rough and smooth.

"See?" Harry said. "Not bad. Soft. That's because we're on the stuff that hasn't happened yet, what would be, to us, the future. Now just wait a sec."

He looked off to the right. "Okay, here it comes."

"Here comes what? Should I duck?"

Before she could, she felt a pop, as if her ears suddenly cleared of water. Everything in her field of vision wavered, briefly out of focus, then steadied again.

"Done," Harry said. "Now, feel the ground again."

She did. It wasn't soft anymore. It was stiff, dry, brittle. She was afraid some powder or something from it would cover her hands, but the "terrain" didn't cling at all.

"Hard, right? That's because the future just happened. It's past. Now look that way." He pointed left. Though nervous at the thought of losing track of him, she turned her head. The trails were everywhere, intersecting, winding, making hills, valleys, even tall mountain ranges. It was all sort of like a big, multicolored bowl of different-size strands of spaghetti, all heading in the same general direction.

"If you look closely, you can see where the future becomes the past. It's like a little heat wave rising from the pavement on a hot day." His finger tracked along the horizon until he found the right spot. "There! Look there!"

A weird fuzzy line, like the fizz on top of a glass of Pepsi, moved slowly away from them in a long strip that ran from horizon to horizon. It was scary but a little thrilling, too.

"I see it," she said.

"Great. You know, I should probably name it too. Maybe the event horizon? Or is that too sci-fi? Anyway, now look around. The trails that are about the size and width of people? They're people—their whole lives from beginning to end, birth, childhood, middle age, all the way to death. They're hard in the past, and I don't think they can change anymore, but the future is soft, more malleable. As people make different choices, their futures shift around, so their trails change. Just one choice can shift a whole bunch of other trails. Right before you shook me out, I saw a really cool ripple when this one woman decided to leave her husband. I think he was abusive, and as soon as she dumped him, everything just perked up for everyone she knew," Harry said. "All their trails straightened up and flew out into tomorrow, thick and strong. They even had a sheen to them, like a healthy dog. It was like she threw a pebble into a stream in just the right spot."

Siara shook her head in disbelief. "You can actually see what happens in people's lives? How? It all looks like a blob of giant pasta to me."

"From here, usually it looks that way to me too. But you if you, um . . . actually go *into* the trail," he said, "things start to make sense. Things pop out from the walls, and after a while you start to just know all sorts of stuff. Even the names of people you've never met. It's like one of those pre-recorded narrators at the zoo explaining the animals."

Animals?

Something whizzed by her head, sending a few plum-red strands across her eye and into her mouth. She pushed her hair back and looked up. The thing that had flown by wasn't an animal exactly; it looked more like a pretty pattern printed on both sides of a sheet of paper. As she pivoted her head to follow it along, she saw more, swooping, rubbing one another, diving. Each was different, like rainbow snowflakes. There was a nice singing sound to them, too.

"I think I'll call those Timeflys," Harry said, apparently on a roll with the whole naming thing. "Because, well, they fly and make a really nice sound, like if you could tune an insect. Plus it's a play on how time flies, you know?"

"Yes, I know. I got it. But what *are* they?" Siara asked.

"No idea," Harry said. As he looked up, a peaceful expression came over his face. "So far, they seem harmless. There's lots of them, all over the place."

At first it had been sort of comforting how easygoing he was about everything here, but it was starting to annoy her. "A-Time, Timeflys. Why are you naming everything? It's not like they're your pets."

"You don't like Timeflys? You want to call them something else?"

She shook her head. "No, it's just kind of . . . weird. I mean, it's not yours, you know. What if they already have names?"

"Maybe they do," Harry said. "But until I find out what they are, naming them makes them easier to think about. Then again, they may *not* have names." He patted himself on the chest. "I may be the first human to come to A-Time. Why shouldn't I name stuff? Adam named all the animals in the garden of Eden. I always wondered how he came up with *aardvark*."

"Oh, please," she said. "Get over yourself. We could both be having a psychotic break."

He pulled her to her feet. "And if you break it, it's yours! Tell you what—look around. You find something new, you name it. It'll make you feel better. Trust me."

She did trust him, sort of. It was herself she wasn't sure about. She was feeling a little giddy being here, being with him, and she didn't know what to make of any of it. "Harry, you seem to understand all this naturally. It just comes to you. But me, I—"

"Oh, come on. Try! It's easy. It's not a rain forest; it's my aunt's lousy old working-class neighborhood. Just mushed up a little."

He had a point. Pursing her lips, she peered about, but whenever her view veered too far from Harry, she got dizzy, so she tried to keep him at least peripherally in sight.

click click click—

A few feet behind him, something long and thin, like a stick, curved over the top of some hilly trails. It was followed by another stick, just like it, then two more; four in all. At first Siara was startled, but the four sticks just sat there, motionless, blending into the terrain like . . . sticks. If she hadn't seen them move, she wouldn't be able to see them at all now. They reminded her of those insects from biology that camouflaged themselves as sticks.

Maybe she should name them? But what? Sticks? That was lame. Maybe something cooler, like styx, after the river Styx from Greek mythology, which separated the land of the living and of the dead, kind of like regular time and A-Time. Or did that sound too much like a snack treat? Cheese styx or tater styx. Or that geriatric rock band?

Well, it's worth a shot, she thought. She pointed to them and said, "Okay, those over there. How about I call those . . ."

click click click—

The things moved again, synchronously, like fingers drumming on a table. In an instant, she realized they weren't separate creatures at all; they were the legs of *one* creature, and they were pulling its horrid round body up over the trail tops with blinding speed. The sticks held up a round head, and the head was mostly mouth, wide-open mouth, with sharp shark teeth. Within the center of the teeth, where a tongue should have been, was a big round eye on a wet, pulpy stalk.

By the time Harry half turned, it had barreled into her and knocked her off her feet, its body the size and weight of a pit bull. She could see now that its four long appendages each ended in a sharp claw. These claws were trying to push her flailing arms out of the way of its mouth, to get its teeth closer to her face.

It's going to eat me!

As she struggled, its eye examined her, looking between the strands of her hair, inside her ears, stretching to wherever there was something to see. All the while, something wet and sticky dripped from the stalk that held it, like saliva.

Siara screeched, not the way she did during a slasher movie, more like the way the girl who was *in* the slasher movie screeched. And she wasn't embarrassed at all, only terrified. The thing, earless, didn't react. She batted at the eye stalk, but the sticky stuff clung to her arm.

The teeth were inches from her face when Harry's hands appeared over and below its jaws, forcing it to clamp its mouth shut. He tugged, and the multiple claws pulled free. Breathless, Siara scrambled to a seated position just in time to watch Harry spin and hurl the thing away.

As it hit the terrain, it curled up into a ball like a pill bug and lay there. Was it dead? No such luck. After a moment, it stood again, none the worse for wear, and began "sniffing" around the terrain, using that horrible eye like a nose. It was, at least, moving away from her.

"Sorry about that," Harry said. "Good thing that one wasn't very strong. I don't think it could've really hurt you."

"What do you mean? Did you see those teeth?" Siara shouted.

Harry moved to cover his ears. "Okay, okay. But think about it. The last time I was here, my body was still in linear time, right? You found me and shook me awake."

"Riiiighhht . . ." Siara said, deep creases forming on her brow.

"So even though we *look* like we have bodies here," Harry said, holding up his hand, "I think we're made up of something else, like an astral projection, spirit or ectoplasm or whatever. So I'm not sure we can be, you know, eaten. Or hurt, even."

"Oh? What if it eats our souls, smart-ass?"

Harry gave her a look. "This isn't *Return of the Mummy*, you know."

Sighing, Siara looked around. "So where *are* our bodies?"

Harry jerked his thumb over his shoulder. "Like I said, back in my aunt's loft." His face turned a little red. "Probably still kissing. Um . . . you okay?"

She checked herself, whatever her self was. It looked like her, same clothes, same body—only now there was icky monster drool on her sleeves. "Am I okay? Define okay."

Changing the subject, he said, "I'm afraid I already named that one anyway. I call it a Quirk. But the really exciting part is, I think I know what it is."

"Whoopee," said Siara, wrestling with her shirt in an effort to wipe off the sticky stuff.

He pointed at the creature. "No, no—look! Watch what it does."

It crawled along a trail, right at the line where the fuzzy thing—the event horizon, in the world according to Harry—indicated the future was becoming past.

"Quirks seem to be made of the same stuff as trails, so maybe a quirk is like a living, disconnected series of events, and all it wants, all it lives for, is to 'happen'—to find an appropriate spot where it fits in. That one, I could tell when I grabbed it, is no big deal—it's just someone dropping their morning mail. Look! It found a spot!"

The eye stalk disappeared into the spongy surface, making the Quirk look like an ostrich sticking its head in the sand. It stiffened, and the rest of the body trembled. Just as the fuzziness passed, it dove in, melting into the trail. It was gone.

"And Mr. Sam Delaney of 2187 Cruger Avenue drops his morning mail. Ta-da! I saw a Quirk form once. When that woman left her husband, one popped out of her trail. I think when someone makes a choice that changes the future, the trails reconnect in ways that leave out a few events—and they pop out as Quirks. Cool, huh?"

"No, it is *not* cool!" Siara was at her limit. The sticky stuff was all over her hands now, refusing to come off. "That thing could have killed me!" she shouted. "This is crazy, all of it! And I'm crazy too! And I don't want to be crazy! My parents want me to go to Yale and become a lawyer, and I don't think they take crazy people!"

"I thought you secretly wanted to be a poet," Harry said softly. "Like Emily Dickinson or Elizabeth Bishop."

Siara's brow furrowed; then she felt her stomach tightening. "What are you talking about? I never told you anything about . . . I've never told *anyone* about . . ."

Realization dawned. Eyes opened wide. A-Time. Trails. *Things start to make sense.* She glared at him. The knot in her stomach grew tighter. There was a swimming sensation in her gut. She was getting nauseous. "Did you look at my life trail?"

God, what would he have seen? What sort of stuff "made sense" to him about her? *It must be like mind reading if he knows about Dickinson and Bishop.* Could he even know how she felt about *him*?

Remorse flashed on Harry's face. His confident look melted into sheepishness. "Uh . . . just a little . . . I left before you took a shower."

"Before I *showered*?" she gasped. "Oh my God, I can't believe you. . . ."

All at once, she started hitting him with her open hands, pummeling his shoulders and arms. When that didn't feel like enough, she balled her hands into fists and pounded his chest. "That's my life! It's none of your business! You stay away from it!"

He guiltily stumbled backward, blocking her blows with his arms.

For the first time since they'd arrived in A-Time, Harry frowned. He looked sincerely guilty. "Sorry, I'm sorry, I'll never do it again, I promise. It was the first trail I was ever in and I didn't even know what would happen. And I swear, I barely saw anything."

She stopped and tried to catch her breath, then nodded. She believed him, but she still didn't want to look at him. So she crossed her arms over her chest and turned away, staring instead at the weird ground.

"Look, I'm really, really sorry," he said again. "But trust me, it wasn't anything bad or even, like, revealing. And if you want to still be angry at me, maybe you should do that later. Right now, maybe you should be, well, looking around here. It's pretty special."

She took a sharp breath, then looked up at A-Time. It was true: what she saw was amazing. The trails were kind of beautiful in a way, almost peaceful. It was sort of like watching ocean waves. She squinted, trying to separate one from the other.

"I shouldn't be speaking to you, you transcendental Peeping Tom, but I'm dying of curiosity," she finally said. "Which one's mine?"

Cautiously, Harry stepped next to her and pointed. "That one. I knew it in a minute. It has such a nice pattern, it really stood out from the rest."

She took that as a compliment. "Can I . . . can I go see my future?"

He shook his head. "I don't think so. I tried it with

mine; didn't work. I think entering your own life trail sets up some kind of feedback loop, like when you hold a microphone next to a speaker and you get a horrible squeal. It just popped me back out."

"Figures," she said.

She noticed there were more Quirks around, scattered along the landscape, some not far away enough for comfort. "Harry, do you think we should start trying to figure out how to get back home?"

"Okay. Sure. But can I show you just one more thing?"

She frowned. "Does it involve something that can bite me?"

"Um . . . yeah . . . there's a Quirk, a big one. But really, they're mostly interested in the trails. I don't think this one will pay any attention to us if we're careful," he said.

She shook her head. "No way."

"We could hide. It's important. It's got to do with what's been going on with me . . . and it kind of finishes our tour . . . or our date . . . or whatever. . . ."

Hmm. It'd been a big day—seeing a gunshot fired, cutting out from school, getting kissed, transcending time. What difference could one more surprise make?

"Can I hide behind you?"

He paused as if thinking about it. "Okay." He took her arm and led her on a short walk. He put his arm around her to steady her as they went. She didn't stop him, but she didn't want him thinking she liked it, either.

After a while, he motioned for her to crouch down.

"See that long, twisted trail, darker than the rest? Kind of like a haunted house on a street full of beautiful houses?"

It was hard to miss. She nodded. "What is it?"

"'Todd Penderwhistle's trail," he said.

7. *Yuck*, thought Siara.

Rough, moldy, and swollen, Todd Pender-whistle's life trail jutted from the terrain like a bruise. It was colored in shades of black and brown with flecks of red, like a rotten apple covered with sores that oozed dark fluid.

Yuck, thought Siara again.

She was relieved to feel Harry's hand on her shoulder, but it wasn't a comforting pat. Apparently she wasn't crouching enough, because he hissed, "Stay down," then, "Look left."

It was hard to tell, because the colors and the textures matched so well, but she thought she could make out something big, round, and fat near the trail. Taller than she was, taller than Harry, wide as a Humvee, it made the other Quirk look like a toy. The saliva dripping from its stalk formed little puddles on the terrain. Its eye, larger than Siara's head, hovered about like a grizzly bear watching a river for fish.

"It was sniffing at the same spot the first time I saw it. I think it's looking for a way into Todd's life," Harry said. "And it senses one might open up soon."

"What'll it make Todd do? Shower?" she said. She was disappointed when Harry didn't laugh.

"It's waiting for him to get depressed enough; then it's going to make him jump out of a window," Harry said plainly.

Despite the sheer repulsiveness of the scene, Siara felt a twinge of pity for the dangerous man-giant.

"Wow. But would it be . . . you know, his choice?" she asked. "Or will it force him?"

Harry's eyes widened. "Free will. Big, big question. I think sometimes people have free will and sometimes they don't. I think Todd has choices up until the quirk connects, but once it wedges itself in there, it's all over. It's really strong, giving off all sorts of . . . I dunno, warning waves. I first sensed it when I saw Todd in study hall. All these weird visions I've been having center on it, like it's got some kind of draw for me, but I can't figure out why. There's also something going on with a pink clown balloon, but I haven't figured that part out yet."

Maybe he's psychic. . . .

Duh! Look around you! Of course *he's psychic. He's psychic-plus. But why would* he *be drawn to Todd?*

When an answer popped into her head, she said it without thinking.

"Maybe you're supposed to stop him."

Harry laughed. "Yeah, right. And maybe I'm secretly suicidal."

Not quite standing, he shuffled closer to the trail.

"Harry? Where are you going?"

"Just one more thing. Inside."

She grabbed his sleeve. "Inside? Inside Todd's life? Aside from the fact that that sounds really gross, won't Mr. Teeth see us?"

"Mr. Teeth? No, no, no. A *Quirk*, Siara," Harry said. He shuffled along, crouching now and again. "And don't worry. We'll enter in his past, then move up to his future. The Quirk won't even know we're there."

She stopped.

I don't want to go in there.

But Harry kept moving.

Then again, I don't want to be out here alone. . . .

So she followed.

The trail curved behind a hill, out of the Quirk's sight. Here Harry scrambled atop the surface of what was otherwise known as Todd's past and pulled Siara along. The trail here was hard, but just as ugly.

"This is kind of tricky," he said. "The first time I tripped and fell in. So maybe we should just sort of dive."

"Dive?" she said, feeling the solid surface with her feet. "Won't it hurt?"

"Surprisingly, no," he said. He took her hand. "It'll

be fastest and easiest if we jump together. On three. One . . . two . . ."

On three, Siara didn't move. She also didn't let go of his hand when he jumped, so that he, along with half her arm, vanished into the trail with a little puff of silvery dust that formed a small circle as it rose. When it vanished, she could see that her arm was embedded in the trail, up to the elbow. Worse, her skin was experiencing all sorts of sensations, like it was surrounded by worms. She tried to yank her arm out, but it stuck fast. Instinctively, she leaned forward to gain leverage, but as her weight pressed down, the trail opened beneath her and she tumbled in headfirst.

After a rush of black and a weightless feeling, she felt Harry try to catch her. They both wound up tangled together on what she assumed was the floor of Todd's life. While having Harry wrapped around her wasn't so bad, it also felt to Siara like she'd entered a filthy men's room, where the stench was overwhelming and only one cheap lightbulb fought the darkness.

As she untangled herself from Harry's body, she flashed back to the kiss that had brought her into all of this. When she thought of the moment, she felt like she was back in it, their lips locked tight. She touched her A-Time lips and wondered at the sensation.

"This way," Harry said. She felt him pull her along. Did he feel it too?

That answer would have to wait. All around her, Todd's

life was popping out of the wall, just as Harry had described. It wasn't like a movie, exactly, though there was a lot of seeing involved. Her other senses were triggered too—hearing, taste, smell. Sometimes they were a blur, but every now and then they fell together into a single scene.

She saw an infant Todd, not at all cute even as a baby, sitting on a bare, water-stained floor. He looked malnourished, smallish wads of baby fat disappearing into flaps of too-thin skin. A torn blanket half covered one leg as he stared numbly ahead. She felt a weird, gross discomfort from a soiled diaper and a dull sense of wonder at the specks of dust the baby watched as they danced in the light.

I'm feeling what he's feeling! Just like Harry said . . .

A furry creature came waddling toward him. Baby Todd gurgled, reaching out a pudgy hand. The baby was pleased by what it saw, its whole body happy all at once. Siara thought it was a dog or a cat, some family pet. But then a strip of sunlight from some broken blinds illuminated brown fur and a pointed nose.

It's a rat! A rat the size of a freaking cat!

Its mouth was open, teeth glistening. Giggling, baby Todd reached for it with his left hand, little fingers splayed. Siara stumbled back, tearing herself free of the feeling.

She was about to scream when she felt Harry behind her, warm and reassuring.

"Try not to look too much," he cautioned. "It's not

very pretty, and if you stare too hard, you start to think Todd's life is happening to you."

As they moved, she tried to look away, but details slipped through—hungry nights unfed, filthy clothes, a cigarette burn for crying too much. She grabbed her arm at that, expecting to touch seared flesh. The feelings were too much.

She felt Harry pull her along faster. He cleared his throat and continued toward the future. "Almost there. In case you're wondering how he got in, here's where he buys the answers to the RAW entrance exam. And here . . . it's today. . . ."

Harry was starting to sound like some sort of surreal tour guide for Todd: The Experience. He stopped and pressed his hands against the wall. "If you look hard right here, you can almost see the ghost of a different future, where the bullet kills Jeremy."

Siara stared. There was the auditorium, just as it had been that morning. Between the chairs Harry had arranged, she saw wispy images, almost like patterns in wood grain that made pictures, pictures you had to believe in to see. In them, when Todd fired, the top half of Jeremy Gronson's head exploded. She winced and looked away.

Harry pointed farther ahead. "It didn't change much for Todd. He still gets tackled by the football team, then escapes the police. . . ."

They took a few more long steps as Todd raced across wide streets, ducked between tall buildings, and laid low in piles of trash. The police lost him long before he gave up running. At last, he stopped long enough to force his long legs between his arms, so at least his cuffed hands were in front of him.

The first time she'd seen him run, she'd felt her fear—now she felt his. Exhausted, he came to a building, old and decrepit. He found the remains of a particular room, sat down, and wept. It was strange to see a monster cry.

"Ungh! Ungh! Ungh!"

The sound startled her. At first she worried it was the Quirk, coming to eat them all, then she realized it was Todd.

He flung his cuffed hands at an exposed pipe, making reptile grunts as he tried to snap the chain between his handcuffs. All he managed was to scrape his skin, and metallic gristle smeared on his sleeves. Frustrated, he slammed his head into the pipe.

"Ungh!"

The pipe was slightly dented, Todd's head bruised, bits of plaster and blood on his nearly bare head.

She could hear him think. Or was it him? It sounded more like something talking *about* him. She remembered what Harry had said about a sort of narrator. It felt like a little god was sitting on Todd's shoulder, whispering into her ear:

The stupid little chain was stronger than it looked, and the small of his back itched like mad. He wished he had his gun. He could shoot the cuffs off.

The high-ceilinged room was bare, patches of floor missing, joints exposed. Whole damn building wobbled like a crack addict. Still, it was home. No one would look for him here. Sure, maybe his childhood address was on some computer, but by the time anyone thought to look, he'd be dead. Live fast, die young, leave a great-looking corpse.

Well, two out of three ain't bad. . . .

But first, he had to get his hands free and scratch that itch. He scrunched his shoulders, hoping to rub the spot with the folds of his muscles, but it didn't work. He looked at the cuffs and wondered if he could yank his hand off.

Maybe he could squeeze his hand through the cuff? The two fingers almost gone might make a difference. If it worked, it'd be the first time his gimpy nubs were an advantage.

Was this the same spot in the room where he'd lost them? Where the rat bit him? Couldn't tell. He wondered if they were still around here, sitting in an old rat's nest behind a wall, little bits of baby bone. Todd chuckled, imagining his skeletal mother racing around this very room with a broom, chasing the big fat rat, shrieking, "Gimme back my baby's fingers!"

If his mother had found the pieces, they could've been sewn back on. But she'd never done any such thing. Hadn't even gotten him to the emergency room for two hours. The doctor had said if the rat hadn't bitten past the first knuckle and the wounds had been cleaned, the fingers could actually have grown back. As it was, they'd said he was lucky to have kept his hand. That was what his mother had said last month during visiting hour at the Highpoint Women's Correctional Facility, aka prison. When he'd asked why she told him, she'd just said, "I dunno," and gotten a funny look in her eye. He'd gotten the same look and the same answer when he asked, "Why did you have me? Why didn't you get an abortion?"

"I dunno."

Did she know what was going to happen to her? Did she know she was going to die?

Stupid goddamn itch!

He made his hand as thin as he could, pressed thumb toward palm, pushed the other fingers into each other. The scraped flesh stung.

Close your eyes, pretend it's Gronson's hand, and pull!

"Yearghh!"

The pain made his tongue fly back against his throat and a gob of phlegm explode in his nose. But rather than sliding free, his left hand was now wedged halfway through the steel ring. More bone than flesh, his half pinky drew blood from the slightly longer remains of his ring finger. The blood didn't bother him, but the bone must have hit a live nerve, and that hurt worse than the itch.

So he pulled again.

"Nghhhhh!"

This time something shredded, broke, and came free. Todd's large form crumpled to its knees. He cradled his bleeding hand, relieved no one was there to see him cry, annoyed there was no one there for him to kill.

Gingerly he pried the pinky from the ring finger. The pain slowed. He slumped against a wall and felt it touch the itchy small of his back. He pressed in and rubbed. His coat bundled in just the right spot and he finally, finally relieved his itch.

Ahhhhh!

Then he clenched his teeth, shook his head, and slammed it back against the wall. He could've just done that hours ago! Avoided crushing his hand! If he'd thought of it. But he hadn't. What an idiot!

Outside, a dark alleyway, some eight stories down, waited. It was enough of a fall to kill anybody. Todd fished for a cigarette, lit it, and drew. The glowing red ember at the tip seemed the only color among all the grays.

He was an idiot. His mother was right. If only the rat had bitten his head, sucked his brains out.

He looked out the window and thought of flying. He'd made up his mind to kill himself the same moment he'd decided to bring the gun to school. Knowing today was his last had given him the guts to shoot Gronson and run from the police.

But jumping seemed too simple. He wanted an assist. Not the usual stuff that just sent his head soaring for a while. For this, Todd wanted a full-body effect, to kill the pain in his hand, make everything else look pretty, and last him all the way down.

Cigarette dangling from his lips, he fished for the throw-away cell phone he'd lifted from the convenience store and punched in the only number he knew.

"Nikoli? Todd. I want to chase the dragon. Yeah, I'm sure. Can you hook me up?"

The voice stopped as quickly as it had started, as if Siara had reached the end of some sort of unit, a chapter or a scene. She felt like she'd stepped back out onto the street after a long, compelling movie.

Harry was a few feet away, waving his hands frantically.

"This way! Over here! Come on!"

He was very excited. So full of life, especially compared to Todd. Her steps feeling leaden, she dragged herself closer to him.

"Thought I'd lost you to Todd for a minute," he said with a funny smile.

She practically fell into his arms, grateful when he hugged her tightly.

"It's okay," he whispered. "We're almost done."

They stood in what looked like an abbreviated fork. In one direction, it ended abruptly with an image of Todd throwing himself out a window. In the other direction, there was a kind of wall. It seemed out of place, but it was hard to say how. It just looked different from everything else.

"I think Todd had some kind of choice here," Harry said. "But globby bits of the terrain cover it, like with

109

plaster, making sure his life goes the other way . . . to the end."

Siara looked around nervously. "Could the Quirk have done it? Maybe to make sure it could happen?"

Great, she thought. *Now I'm starting to talk like Harry.*

He shook his head. "Don't think so. They're really animal. I'm pretty sure they can't even get into the trails unless they're occurring. Then once they happen, they become part of the walls. Maybe . . . maybe when Todd fired that gun today it eliminated this possibility, but I'm not so sure."

He pressed against the surface. It gave a bit, then hissed.

"I wish I could see what would've happened," Harry said. "Part of me really wants to know. It's got something to do with the visions I've been having."

"Harry, what's 'chasing the dragon?'"

He looked at her quizzically. "I think it's a way of taking heroin. You put the powder on foil and heat it with a lighter. The heroin turns to a sticky liquid and wriggles around like a dragon. Then you inhale the fumes, I guess. I saw it in a movie about the Yakuza once. Why?"

"Something Todd said he wanted to do. I saw it in the trail," she said.

"Huh. I missed that part. I guess we see different things. Cool," Harry said. He slapped his hands against his pants. "Well, that brings us to the end of the tour. Gift shop on your left, where you can purchase Todd T-shirts and cigarette lighters."

They walked quietly but quickly back to the spot where they'd come in. Harry climbed out and pulled a confused Siara back to the surface. *Why did he show me all that? Why, of all the millions of trails in A-Time, was he drawn to that one?*

She didn't have time to ponder it. The Quirk was waiting for them. Harry vanished instantly when it wrapped two appendages around him, lifted, and threw. His form skittered across the terrain, bouncing like a stone on water. The Quirk, taken off balance by the throw, righted itself and turned to Siara. It towered over her, showing its teeth and a single, bloodshot eye. Its mouth alone was half the size of her body.

She screamed, going cold.

As she searched for a place to run, she caught a glimpse of Harry getting to his feet. He barreled back as the Quirk was about to snap its mouth shut around her and slammed into her side, taking them both out of the way. She got to her feet first and started pulling Harry along.

"Come on! Come on!" she said.

She heard Harry pant as they ran, whether from panic or exhaustion, she couldn't tell. She looked back. The Quirk was gaining.

"What's it want with us?" Siara cried.

"I don't know! Maybe it saw us poking around Todd's trail. Maybe it thinks we want to steal its food!" Harry said.

They slipped behind a high rise of trails, a swelling that formed a high, angular hill, like a rocky outcropping.

"Can't we just go back home?" she asked.

"Love to. How?"

The Quirk's eye rounded the corner, blinked at them, then brought its huge body along with it. She and Harry took off again. As the ground beneath her grew more solid, she realized they were in the past, where the terrain was less even.

Harry looked like he recognized something.

"What?" Siara said.

"They can't go into the trails in the past. At least I don't *think* they can go into the trails in the past," he said, puffing. He pulled her close to a spot on the hard ground. "You hide down here. I'll . . . I'll lure it away or something," he said.

"I can't stay here!" she said.

"You wouldn't *be* here if it weren't for me. I know what I'm doing. Trust me."

"What if I trust that you *don't* know what you're doing?"

She looked down at the trail under her feet.

"Whose life is this, anyway?"

"Mine. I figure this will make us even for when I saw your life, okay?" he said.

The Quirk nearly upon them, Harry roughly shoved her. Unable to stop herself, she went down, down beneath the psychedelic surface and into Harry Keller's personal dark.

8. *Well, this totally sucks,* Harry thought as the Quirk chased him across the rugged landscape.

He did feel really good about getting Siara to safety, like he'd done the right thing, maybe even the manly thing, but the sensation didn't last when he realized he had no idea how to save himself. If he was right, and the Quirk just wanted to scare them away from Todd's trail, it should've lost interest in him by now. But it hadn't.

He had to put more distance between them, but how? He needed a plan, badly, but all his supposedly brilliant mind could come up with was, "Run! Run! Run!"

See Harry run. Run, Harry, run!

He thought of jumping into a trail, any trail, but if he was wrong and the Quirk followed, it could make some poor sucker kill himself.

Once again, he silently thanked his dead father for his ethics.

He looked back over his shoulder. The Quirk's four clawed appendages grabbed the spaces between trails and yanked the hefty body along at a blinding rate. The hardness of the past seemed to help its mobility, allowing

114

the spidery thing to gain momentum. Harry's own feet, meanwhile, were starting to hurt.

A plan, a plan.

The future's springy, like a trampoline. If I can make it there, maybe I can bounce away from it!

It sounded stupid enough to work. The event horizon was visible far to his left, but Harry was headed into the past. Unfortunately, the Quirk was too close for him to risk turning. Then came a new surprise.

It pursed its ghastly lips and said, "Unk! Unk!"

Oh, great, now it's making noise. . . .

It sounded like a sickly, giant goose.

On the brighter side, as the terrain underfoot grew more uneven, the inclines, declines, and ridges seemed to slow it. But why didn't it go away? Had it smelled something tasty on him? *Could* the ugly thing smell?

"Unk! Unk! Unk!"

Concentrate! What's around me?

A few yards ahead, an irregular trail jutted up, making a shape somewhere between a tree and a playground monkey bar. As Harry ran by the outgrowth, he grabbed it and spun, quickly shifting his direction.

"Unk!"

Just as Harry let go, the Quirk hit the outgrowth hard. Its long, spindly legs splayed out under it. It splatted down on the terrain like a gargantuan mottled grapefruit.

"Unk!"

115

Thinking he'd have some time before the Quirk righted itself, Harry took his gaze off the creature and picked up speed. Directly ahead he saw the familiar fuzzy line. A few more strides and he'd be in the future, hopefully bouncing along to safety. No sooner did Harry breathe a sigh of relief than his foot caught on something. He tripped and fell forward.

"Crap!" he said aloud.

The terrain hit him like a pile of cardboard. His hands dipped into a trail, but he managed to yank them out and push himself to his knees. Before he could fully stand, a large eye slithered into his face, then popped him in the chest, pushing him back down.

"Unk," the Quirk said.

He was right under it, and he wasn't going anywhere. In a few seconds, when it tore into him, he'd learn what he was really made of in A-Time: immortal spirit, like Siara suggested, or some form of yummy flesh that tasted really good to a Quirk.

Siara—she was all about the soul thing. He wished he could see her. Even as the Quirk pressed down, the thought of their first kiss popped into his mind, far more welcome than his usual stray thoughts.

First and *last kiss,* he thought.

With Quirk claws on him and monster-teeth so real and near, her face melted as more pragmatic thoughts came to his mind, thoughts like, *I wonder what it's like to die.*

The thought was too familiar. It felt tense and bubbling in the pit of his stomach, spidery and nagging at the back of his head. It went as deep as the bones the Quirk wanted to chew.

Death, the consequence of time. You can solve it, Harry.

The soul thing.

It seemed, even to him, a strange thing to be thinking as a monster sat on his chest, but he couldn't shake the Quirk or the thought.

Does everyone spend so much time thinking about dying, or is it me? And if it's me, how did I get this way?

Siara's first thought was to help Harry whether he liked it or not, then give him a good swift kick for shoving her out of the way. But she had to be honest about it: the A-Time swirl was making her really dizzy. Every time she tried to pull herself up and out of the tunnel, vertigo hit. After she'd failed three times, a gentle melody, half hummed, teased away any thoughts of leaving.

What was that sound, and where was she, anyway, in Harry's life? This place wasn't like Todd's icky trail at all—it was eclectic, weird, full of twists and turns, but there was a kind of serenity and strength to it—things she wouldn't have guessed Harry capable of, at least after his freak-out.

So why do *I like him?*

Images rose: A woman in a frayed blue bathrobe sat on an old chair by a white box crib, rocking her newborn. Stray threads from her robe mixed with her corn-silk hair. She was singing—that was the sound Siara heard:

The last time I saw you
Was now
The next time I see you
Will always be now
I may not always love you
I may not know how
But oh, how I love you now

Siara would've dismissed it as sappy, but somehow she knew the woman had written it herself. That made it seem terribly cool.

A fellow poet . . .

With the ever-present despair that had been in Todd's trail absent here, Siara started to enjoy the experience a little. It wasn't quite as dark or as scary. There was even a general aura of happiness in the air.

This is kind of neat. And Harry's such a cute widdle baby! Aw!

But then a tall, thin man appeared at the nursery door, hands large, shoulders lanky. As he drifted into the light, he seemed more familiar, particularly the knitted brow. From the hesitant gait and fumbling hands, she realized it was Harry's dad. That narrator thing whispered his name: Frank, Frank Keller. And the woman was Jennifer.

118

And the sense of joy just vanished, like water in the sand.

Frank wasn't coming in. He wavered at the door, stuck, a terrific fear holding him back, while an equally powerful longing tried to push him in.

Jennifer's song finished, she sensed her husband's presence and turned to smile at him. She was wan, tired, but happy. Frank forced a smile but wouldn't go to her or to his child. He told himself he didn't want to hurt the scene with his presence, with the pain he felt inside, but he was really just afraid.

Feeling like an eavesdropper, Siara moved on. What was Frank afraid of? He should've been thrilled—new baby, beautiful wife. More light, more dust, and a heavy somberness rose.

Oh.

A funeral parlor folded out from the wall. Cheerful Muzak piped through the viewing room like party balloons at an accident scene. People dressed in black shifted sadly in brown folding chairs. Jennifer Keller was the one in the white box now. The top half of her coffin was open, the texture of her face all wrong, her cheeks painted a ghastly red.

Siara raised a hand to her lips, remembering that Harry's mother had died soon after he was born.

That was why his dad was afraid. She was sick. She was dying. Was it cancer?

Another scene rose. Nighttime, back in the nursery.

Frank still had on his black suit, but the tie was loosened. Harry was in his crib, watching his father sling a set of tiles across the wooden bars. A night lamp threw the tiles' square shadows on the wall. Siara could see that they showed the alphabet and the numbers.

Frank Keller touched each one, repeating its name over and over as Harry watched.

"A-B-C-D-E-F-G, 1-2-3-4-5-6-7."

The baby's eyelids drooped, hungry for sleep, but his father jostled him awake, trying not to be too rough. He pointed to the tiles again.

"A-B-C-D-E-F-G, 1-2-3-4-5-6-7.

"God does not play dice with the universe. You'll figure it out, Harry," he said. "You'll do great things. Save the world. Give her death some meaning. Tomorrow I'll get you some science tapes. . . ."

Siara again felt the fear in the man. She was surprised that it didn't feel selfish, like Todd's or even her own, but it did feel more desperate, obsessive.

Frank Keller didn't care about himself. He just didn't want his wife to be dead. He just didn't want to know that one day his son would be dead. He just did not want death. Death didn't make any sense to him, none at all, and God's universe, he believed, had to make sense.

"For now we see through a glass, darkly; but then face to face: now I know in part; but then shall I know even as also I am known," he said. He parsed each word with a longing that trumped his lack of charisma.

Years later, Frank Keller's black jacket sliced the air as he pivoted in a large basement room, sizing up the crowd that had gathered to listen to his rejection of death. In one large hand, he clasped a small Bible. His fear had hidden behind it and made itself holy.

Listeners bobbed their heads. Seven-year-old Harry sat near his father, acting like he understood.

"That was Paul, in First Corinthians. He tells us quite plainly that understanding is salvation, that life only seems chaotic because we look through that dark glass, that filthy filter, born of habit and laziness, that clouds our view. It tells us what to pay attention to and what to ignore, what has meaning, and what is in vain. But it lies! Because no life is in vain, no death pointless. In this gracious, giving world, all makes sense."

He slapped the Bible with the flat of his hand. There were nods and a cough here and there.

"Why can't we see past our filters, past ourselves? Why, if it had a reason, does the memory of my wife's death only bring me pain? Why are we tormented? Why does it seem the world fails us?"

He raised his voice again. "Because it is we who fail the world! We who fail God!"

Flecks of spit flew from his mouth. Young Harry raised an arm to block himself from the spray.

"Our only hope is to take that pain, to use it to force ourselves not down into the dark, but up into the light, to force ourselves to that holy understanding, to

121

discover the sense of God's world. In this way, I have taken my only son and tried to give him a keen, sharp mind in the hope that one day he will do what I cannot."

Get over it, Frank.

Angry, Siara stopped listening to the little narrator god. She pressed forward, moving faster and faster, hoping to reach the end of the elder Keller's speech, but it went on and on, for days and years, in different rooms, different places, before different lonely crowds. It was always about making sense, that things had to make sense. And when he wasn't telling a crowd, he was telling Harry.

She saw the small nursery again. It'd been converted, with bookcase, desk, and bed. Through the window, an eggy sun rose and fell, again and again, days passing as if she were scanning forward on a DVD.

Harry sat at the desk, ten or twelve, looking pretty much like Harry. Books were piled high next to him. His head twitched as he read and wrote, then read and wrote, then read and wrote some more. All the while his father paced behind him, chanting, partly to himself, partly to his son, "It's got to make sense; it just has to make sense."

She couldn't believe what the man had been doing to his own son, to Harry. She'd read about wacko parents training children in the cradle to be geniuses and how the kids wound up maladjusted, unhappy, totally. . . *crazy.*

But Frank was different: he didn't want Harry to

win prizes or acclaim; he wanted Harry to do what he couldn't, to figure out the thing that terrified him, the consequence of time—death. And Harry, well, Harry was different too. Rough on the edges, twitching, but there was still something inside him, something she really—

Oh!

She wished she could yank him out of there, show him a place to hide, but she couldn't. Years passed. Harry's face elongated, thickened, but still twitched. The pile of books changed. Sometimes it was taller, sometimes shorter, but it never disappeared. For the longest time a cracker and some cheese sat on a plate next to Harry, but he never seemed to eat them, until finally the plate just faded away.

Gray hairs and a paunch appeared on his father, but his movements, his words changed less and less: "It's got to make sense. It just has to make sense."

He said it so often, the words stopped sounding like words. They became just . . . sounds, and then not even sounds. He said it so often, it stopped making any sense at all.

He said it so often, he was beginning to make *death* look good.

"Unk!"

The suicide quirk's teeth pressed closer. Viscous liquid slid in long silvery strands onto Harry's hair and face. Harry, flat on his back and hopelessly outweighed, had somehow stopped the mouth inches away from him. His hands were wedged in the crook of the huge jaw, in a small spot between the shark-like teeth. The fit was so tight it hurt his hands, but he couldn't let go. His elbows were locked. If the quirk pushed any harder, he was sure both arms would snap.

But while there's life, there's hope! Or at least metabolic reactions. This can't be so hard. All I have to do is push the Quirk off while keeping its mouth from clamping shut around the upper half of my body. I could do that easily, if only I were, like, ten times stronger and totally invulnerable. . . .

"Aghh!" Harry said out loud. The Quirk squeezed its jaws tighter. Harry felt like his fingers would pop off.

He shook his head to clear the Quirk spit out of his eyes. He wondered what would happen when, if, he let go. Would it swallow his A-Time self? What would happen to his body back in linear time? Would *he* be the one to plummet to the floor of the alley, not Todd?

He'd been joking before, with Siara. Now he really wondered. Could the Quirk have chased him because it sensed something suicidal in him? Dr. Shapiro was always asking him about suicidal thoughts. Even Tippicks had said he should watch out for the warning signs. Harry had figured they were nuts.

But look who's calling the kettle black. . . .

Were they right?

No! I'm not suicidal! Everything has to make sense!

"Unk!" The Quirk blasted something like air into his face and pushed closer. Harry grunted back, trying to hold his ground.

The eye stalk studied the scene, looking for some weakness. It found one.

It stretched out even farther from the mouth, like a long boa constrictor, and slowly wrapped its sticky wetness around Harry's left wrist. It tensed, squeezing tighter and tighter. Harry felt the pain, every bit of it. Just when it tightened so hard he was sure it couldn't tighten any more, it did.

Then it started pulling. Harry felt his grip loosening, his hand giving way.

"Unk!" It sounded disgustingly satisfied.

Everything has to make sense. . . . It has to. . . .

Inside Harry, the funny line between imagining and experiencing wavered. He saw cracked wet asphalt rush uncontrollably at him, a clown balloon float at his back. Only this time, Todd wasn't falling to his death; it was Harry. The alley was opening up beneath Harry Keller, ready to swallow him forever.

Though Frank Keller mostly preached in the city, at times he was invited to speak upstate, to congregations sympathetic to his ideas about how best to approach the Lord. Word of his passionate speeches spread so far that a big tent had to be set up to accommodate the crowds, and people actually drove great distances to see him.

Frank was terrified whenever he spoke, but his rage forced him past his fear. He didn't think he could really help any of the people who came to listen. It was too late for them, but he did it all anyway, for the benefit of his son. So that Harry would understand how important it was that he be obeyed.

As Siara saw the rows of cars parked on grass and mud, she had to wonder, *Don't these people get cable?* But there was something freeing about the countryside. Here, even in the walls of a life trail, the sky was a vast blue thing, almost as big as all A-Time, with only two thick clouds occupying the center of the celestial stage.

"Understanding is all that makes us human!"

Here we go again!

She knew she was getting near the end. Harry was in RAW, and this was last summer, the summer of his legendary freak-out. Having stuck it out this long, she figured she could take another *everything must make sense!* or two if it helped her, well, make some sense of Harry. She knew Harry's father would die soon, and she couldn't help but want to see how.

As Frank Keller screamed and stormed about, the shadows of two huge clouds settled over the tent, bringing a welcome, cooling shade.

"Understanding is all that makes us safe!"

The temperature dipped by five degrees. Even Harry

relaxed a little, and a slight smile crossed his lips.

When his father noticed, he got angry, as if Harry's smile meant he wasn't paying attention, as if Frank had lost a competition. He held his little Bible as high as he could without standing on his toes.

"Understanding is all we have to live for, and if I am not telling the truth, may God strike me down where I stand!" he screeched.

It was cliché, but heartfelt. As was, perhaps, the miracle that followed.

A bright light, like a huge camera flash, hit the center pole. Soundless, it tore through the tent's thick fabric, slammed down through the static air and into the flesh and blood of Frank Keller, whose hand and Bible were still raised. Briefly, the lightning made him look like a neon sign.

It wasn't until a full second later, before the shock even started to register, that they all heard the thunder, a low, hollow boom—because light travels faster than sound.

It would almost have been funny to Siara, if it weren't for two things. The first was the smell of burnt flesh, like sweet meat sizzling on a barbecue. It made her want to vomit. She heaved, but nothing came up. The second thing was worse: she felt Harry's entire being shudder, then collapse into a dozen little shards, as if he had just witnessed the death of God.

Frank Keller didn't die all at once. There were police cars, a fire truck, and an ambulance; a local emergency room, surgery; then three long days, during which Harry never left a little gray folding chair that at the side of his father's hospital bed.

His father weakened steadily, drinking little, eating less, speaking in fewer words of fewer and fewer syllables, until finally there was only the steady beeping of some machine or another and a gentle rasp of clockwork breath.

Still Harry sat there, hour after hour, expecting, based on what the doctors told him, that at some point the beeping, the heartbeat, would simply stop—like the last note of a song.

Once, just once, he went to the bathroom. When he returned, a nurse was there, pulling off the tube that fed oxygen into his father's nose. The beeping was gone. So were the labored breaths.

It seemed it was all over.

Harry staggered into the hall and tried to memorize the pattern in the linoleum, especially the little metal shards. Numbness took him down the hall to a phone, where he stood for fourteen minutes, trying to think of someone to call. But he couldn't think of anyone, so he went back to the room, just to make sure it had all really happened.

The nurse was still there, hovering. The oxygen was back on, the tube wrapped once again around his father's head. The nurse was intent, listening to his father's motionless chest with a stethoscope.

Harry stared at her.

She whispered, "I thought I heard a heartbeat."

She motioned Harry closer. "Sometimes even after the heart loses its rhythm, it still beats now and again. It doesn't do anything. The person's dead, but. . . I just wanted to be sure."

Harry looked at his father, then at the nurse.

"Can I . . . hear?"

She handed him the stethoscope eartips. He put them on, feeling like a curious child inhabiting the junkyard of an otherwise anesthetized soul.

He listened. There was nothing, then a faint thump, like someone taking a single heavy step far off down a hall. Then nothing for a while. Then another faint thump. No rhyme, no reason. No one to say it had to make sense. Even the rhythm was gone.

"You suck!" Harry screamed at the Quirk.

"Unk!" the Quirk shouted back, sending a huge glob of saliva into Harry's open mouth. He nearly choked trying to spit it out.

Lying beneath it, Harry made a sound somewhere between a laugh and a sob. The eye stalk still yanked at his hand. The bottom row of teeth still inched nearer to his chin. His hands were still wedged at the edges of its mouth.

Reflexively he pulled at the hand held at the wrist by the meaty eye stalk. It gave, just a bit, and the creature seemed to wince.

Hey! Harry thought, furrowing his brow. Previously the stalk had felt adamantine.

An idea wafted through the neurons in Harry's brain, navigating the maze of awful endings he'd imagined for himself. Rather than fight it, Harry reached for it, not so much with desperation but more out of a sense of *What the hell, why not? If I've got to die, I might as well go down trying. . . .*

He pulled his right hand free from the crook of the jaw, then wrapped it around the eye stalk. Now his left arm was the only thing holding back the mouth, but in the new position he could suddenly let go and use both hands to pull the stalk, which he did, for all he was worth. The tongue resisted briefly, then it shot forward just as the quirk pulled back and clamped its mouth shut.

The Quirk missed Harry's nose by inches, biting deep into its own stalk tongue.

"Gerowlf!" it howled.

It sprang up and down, yowling.

"Gerowlf! Gerowlf!"

It clamped its mouth shut and started rubbing itself into the terrain, as if trying to wipe off the pain.

Ha! That's got to hurt.

Had he blinded it? He didn't hang around to find out. He stumbled, ran, then dove behind a huge bump in the trails, into a bed of floating colors that looked like flowers.

He rolled onto his back and saw the quirk race off,

still howling, back in what Harry thought was the direction of Todd's trail.

He'd done it. He and Siara were safe for now. It would have been horrible if anything had happened to her just because she believed in him.

She does believe in me, doesn't she?

He didn't even have enough time to properly congratulate himself when another sound made him lift his head.

"What do you call those?" a voice said, appearing behind him. It was Siara. She pointed at the funny colors he was lying in. Apparently she'd figured out how to climb out of his life trail.

He shook his head, happy to see her. He scrambled to a sitting position as she knelt down beside him.

She seemed a little different. Less dizzy. More gentle. There was a funny look in her eyes. Before he could brag about what he'd done, she cupped his face in her hands and pressed her lips to his forehead.

Pleased, but as always a little confused, he looked into her eyes with a half smile and said, "Wha?"

"I was just wondering if we could get back the same way we got in," she said.

Then she kissed him again, on the lips.

9. The diner was small, a single row of tables and a counter. The late lunch/ early dinner crowd was even smaller, and no one ever really paid attention to what teenagers had to say anyway. Comforted by the inattention of the adults, Harry spoke freely, his mood better than it'd been for a very, very long time.

"I figure for our next date we should probably just go to a movie or something, you know, instead of transcending time."

"Are we dating now?" Siara teased, pushing her hair behind her ears.

He made a face of mock indignation. "Well, if we're not, you're paying for that veggie burger."

She went quiet, a funny expression spreading across her features.

Harry bit his lip, kicking himself for taking it too far. Now that they were out of A-Time, Harry could already feel the confidence and energy he'd had there start to fade. Stray thoughts again poked into his mind. Increasingly nervous about her silence, he scratched his head and fiddled with his napkin.

"Look, it's okay. I mean, the kisses were an experiment, right? But a pretty good experiment, huh? Some people only see stars when they kiss. . . ."

Oh, crap, he suddenly realized. *What if every time I kiss her we wind up in A-Time? That would suck!*

Siara finally broke her silence. "It's not that. I feel like *I* should pay for *you,* the way you've had to . . ."

What does she mean? Why should she have to—Oh.

"The way I live, you mean. The squalor stuff," he said. "Because I'm poor."

She winced. "It's not that. It's . . . your whole life. I thought I had it hard because my parents want me to be a lawyer or a doctor, but you, your dad was like Dr. Frankenstein. He wanted you to be some kind of supercomputer dedicated to discovering the purpose of life."

Harry bristled, surprising himself. "He wasn't so bad! At least he was around. Lots of people don't have anyone. And he taught me a lot. Never would have found A-Time without him. So I twitch a little, big deal. Who's to say it's not biological, maybe even from my mother's side? Besides, how do you know what my dad was like, anyway? You never even met him."

Then it dawned on him. She had. He was so happy they'd survived the Quirk, he'd totally forgotten she'd seen his life. Had she heard his most private thoughts? Harry himself didn't even know what they were.

"So . . . what . . . uh . . . how much . . . how much did you see?" he asked.

She took a bite of burger and pushed a piece of bun into her mouth. "Well . . . how much did you see in *my* life?"

He stared. "No fair. I asked you first."

"You were in *my* life first."

"I already told you, it was only a few minutes! It was my first trail. I saw you wake up, I saw you in school just before we met today, then I left!"

She scrunched her lips together, took his hands, and held them. "I saw a little more than that. I saw how your dad died."

He almost pulled away.

"I'm really, really sorry, Harry. It was awful."

He clenched his jaw. Suddenly he understood why she'd reacted the way she had to the fact that he'd seen her life trail. It was just so . . . *personal*. He looked at her, trying to read her expression. He didn't want her pity, but that wasn't all he saw in her eyes—there was something else, something that kept him from pulling his hand away.

"Yeah. It was," he said finally. "I felt . . . well, you probably know how I felt better than I can say."

He forced a little smile and gently rolled the top of

one of her fingers between his thumb and index finger. Her skin was so soft.

"Yeah, I felt some of what you went through." She stopped, seeming to debate whether to say anything more. Then she took a deep breath, gave his hands a squeeze, and sat back, crossing her arms over her chest. "But maybe we should focus on now. . . . Are you still having visions and stuff back here?"

He looked around. The old couple in the next booth stayed the same age. The cash register didn't move by itself. Everything seemed to be happening one thing at a time, one moment following the next. "So far, so good," he said.

"So, shouldn't we . . . *should* we call the police? About Todd? Tell them where he is?" she asked.

Why'd she bring that *up?*

"What would we say? You want to explain A-Time to Sergeant O'Malley? Besides, we don't even know where Todd is."

"It looked like the same room he was in as a baby, the one with the rat . . ." she said.

She was smart, smarter than Harry had realized. He liked that.

"You saw that too, huh? Certain things just stick out from the trails. It's that narrating thing. Probably worth a name. Drama pops? Nah. Do you have a pen?" Harry started fidgeting in his pockets. "It's important to write this stuff down."

And important to stop talking about saving Todd. I'm happy to be alive right now, thank you.

Siara flashed her fingers in front of his face to get his attention. "Harry, what good is all this knowledge if you can't *help* people?"

He poked his hands in various pockets. "Now you sound like my dad—the guy you called Dr. Frankenstein? You probably missed the part where he was always giving the spare bed to recovering addicts and homeless people. Did you see the time he nearly killed himself saving a handicapped guy from a truck? The man did not believe in triage."

"Triage?"

Okay, so there are still a few things I can tell her.

"It's what doctors do in ERs or at accident scenes. They divide people into three groups: those that get better by themselves, those that need help to get better, and those who won't get better no matter what. Todd's that last variety. Save him today, he kills himself tomorrow, or, worse, he kills someone else. I know you want to do some good, Siara, and that's great, but this isn't it. Think of it as preemptive inaction."

"You said yourself you were curious about what his other future was like."

"I'm curious about a lot of things."

She held up a pen from her book bag. He snatched it and started scribbling on a napkin. From the corner of his eye, he watched her watch him as she rolled a plum-red strand of hair around her index finger.

"What did your mom do?" she asked. "I heard her sing a song."

He pretended to keep writing. "She was a poet," he said. "Like you."

He felt her lean forward for a closer look at his scribbling. Her face made the air around him warmer.

"I wish I could write like that," she said.

He tore off the blank half of his napkin, slid it in front of her, and put the pen into her hands. "You can, you know. Go ahead. Finish your poem."

"Now?"

"Good a time as any."

"I'm too distracted."

"Hey, you think like that, you'll talk yourself out of doing *anything*. Go ahead."

She laughed and crumpled her half of the napkin. "Make you a deal: you save Todd and I promise I'll finish my poem."

"Why is that so important to you?"

"I don't know that it is. I just think it's important to *you*."

Harry slumped in his seat. "How about *I* finish your poem and *you* save Todd?"

"Would if I could."

Harry sighed. *My brain keeps coming back to it, too. Otherwise why be so eager, with all of A-Time around, to show Siara that cesspool of a life? It's got to mean something.*

137

"Well . . . I suppose we could try to get the Quirk away from him," he offered. "But the only person I know big enough to grapple with that puppy is the Todd-meister himself, and even if we found him, I have no idea how to get him to A-Time. I really don't think he'd let me kiss him."

She laughed. It was his first joke that she really, really laughed at.

He was about to laugh back when a familiar flash of pink, visible through the filthy diner window, nabbed his eye. The clown balloon floated into view, its long string dangling down. Harry couldn't take his eyes off it. Siara's bubbly laugh stopped.

"I feel like I'm always asking, Harry, but are you okay?"

Her voice sounded a million miles away.

As if alive, the balloon floated through a small crowd and started hovering by three young, grungy men, maybe all in their twenties. Their sharp cheek-bones and pale skin were similar, like they were family. All wore ill-fitting sweat suits, filthy and torn, pants and tops mixed in color. The tallest walked a half step ahead, flanked on the left by a bulldog of a man with wide, sculpted arms and on the right by a thin, limping man with skeletal hands and a beige cap pulled tight over a small skull. They moved as a unit, dangerous brothers. No one you'd want to mess with. Harry felt threatened just looking at them.

The dread clown on the balloon twisted its lips into

a wider smile. Harry felt his legs go limp, as if he were being asked to dive out of an airplane without a parachute, and pressed his shaking hands flat on the table to hold himself up.

"Outside. Three guys," he whispered. "The triage trio. Won't get better no matter what you do. Can't miss 'em. I am feeling a distinct Todd-ness about them. They've got something to do with his suicide."

Siara's face fell. "Oh my God. They look like serious thugs. Can you tell anything else?"

As they marched out of his view, things got worse.

"Only that I need . . . help. . . ."

He twisted sideways and fell to the floor.

Siara's hands were on him at once, shaking him. He could feel the fear in her fingers. "Harry! Harry!" she said.

Hazy white ceiling panels filled his vision. The raspy voice of the waitress boomed, "Is your friend okay? Want me to call an ambulance?"

He turned in time to see that she was dialing. Sweat dripped from his face. He probably looked like he was dying.

"No ambulance . . ." Harry whispered weakly to Siara. "Get me out of here."

"My God, Harry, look at you! You need help!"

"Please, just do it!"

"Can you even walk?" she said. He felt her arms pull his elbows.

Harry tried to focus. Everyone in the diner turned to look. Some seemed ready to get up to help, others averted their eyes.

"Get me to the door. Get me outside," Harry begged. "Fast."

"I'm trying, but you've got to help a little!" Siara said.

With a grunt, he rolled into a half squat and moved bit by bit toward the exit. No one moved to stop or help them. They all looked stunned.

As Siara opened the door and air hit Harry's face, he saw the three men again. They were cutting a path through a light shopping crowd of old women and teens. As soon as he saw them, he was suddenly strong enough to get to his feet.

A siren wailed. It couldn't be for him, it was way too fast, but the sound panicked him. He steadied himself quickly and marched down the block in the same direction as the trio.

"Feeling better, feeling better," Harry said, forcing a smile. "No ambulance for me. No, sirree!"

Siara broke into a trot to keep up. "Should we follow them?" she asked.

He stopped so quickly Siara bumped into him. "Follow? No! What? Are you kidding? They're like Todd Penderwhistle, only different shapes and sizes."

As the three turned a corner, Harry's legs buckled. His flailing hands grabbed at Siara's corduroy jacket.

The waitress was in front of the diner, scanning the crowd for them. The siren was getting louder. Maybe it *was* for him.

"Help me get away from here," Harry said.

Siara pulled him the rest of the way to the corner. Once the motley trio was back in view again, a block away now, Harry recovered instantly.

"Detecting a pattern," Harry said. "As long as I see them, I'm okay."

"Then we've *got* to follow them," Siara said.

We, Harry thought. He liked the way it sounded, but his father's ethics rose. *I can't put her in danger.*

"Not we. Me," he said. "You've done enough. I'll be fine. Really."

He was sure he sounded brave and competent until a passing truck blocked his view of the sauntering men. Then his eyes rolled up into his head and he fell into Siara's arms like a rag doll.

"Yeah, you're a regular Jeremy Gronson," she said, grunting from the weight.

Despite the throbbing in his head and the wrenching sensation in his gut, Harry somehow managed to find the strength to be offended.

"Hey, we're not *that* different. He's only captain of the debate team because I wigged out. He could never beat me. Try though he might," he said, wincing.

"Okay, okay. Sheesh. Sorry."

"You like the big football type?"

"Forget it, will you? I'm just saying it looks like we're in this together. You need help and here I am."

Harry managed a smile.

"Okay, but if we survive, you owe me the rest of your poem," he said weakly.

"Deal."

They half hobbled to the next block. Spotting his targets again, he straightened and started jogging along to catch up.

Soon they left the safe confines of his working-class neighborhood. Things were less familiar, the faces unknown, and even the distant buildings held no landmarks. Alarm bells went off in his head. In the city, even a few blocks could mean the difference between a comfy home zone and getting mugged.

The people thinned to nearly nothing. A block later, the only person present, other than Harry, Siara, and the guys they were chasing, was an old woman pushing a cart full of bottles of water. They sloshed as she pushed, and she shushed them as they did.

Seeing what was ahead of them, Harry gave the old woman a dollar.

"It's like a nickel for the ferryman," he explained to Siara. "For when you cross into the land of the dead."

"Nice. So we're crossing into the land of the dead now?"

"Yup," he said. He nodded forward.

A half-hung, decades-old sign, rotting with rust,

proudly proclaimed a low-income building project. Beyond it was a vast emptiness—a sea of half-dug holes and concrete nothingness, interspersed with piles of dirt rendered gray by coming night. There was nothing living. The aged construction site looked like the moon, and the moon really sucked.

Standing at its edge, it occurred to Harry, maybe for the first time, that the sad little linear world could be just as strange and dangerous as A-Time.

The trio pushed their way through a hole in the chain-link fence and went inside. Harry and Siara followed, ducking behind garbage cans, backhoes, and mounds of dirt as they strode across the barren landscape and exited near a row of ancient town houses. Half the buildings there had either been torn down or had fallen of their own accord. To Harry, the whole block looked like a mouth with missing teeth.

By the time he and Siara felt comfortable enough to likewise exit the site, night had arrived in earnest, bringing with it a bone-deep chill. It was nearly impossible to see anything, especially since none of the streetlights were working.

"Where is this?" Siara whispered, huddling closer to Harry for warmth. He liked that part.

"Gunning Road, I think," Harry offered. He put his arm around her and felt her shiver from the cold and the sound of the name. Everyone in the city knew the area, the same way everyone knew Coca-Cola or hell. A decade ago, Gunning Road had been a haven for dealers and addicts, a place even the police didn't visit. In the nineties, there were a few urban renewal projects, like the one they'd passed, but after the Internet boom went bust, so did the renewal. These days Gunning Road was believed empty, except for wild dog packs and cat-size rats.

Harry pulled Siara's head closer. "Still want to change Todd's destiny?"

"S-s-sure. Just c-c-cold now," she said. "You?"

Harry shook his head. "If I wasn't doing a major freak-out every time those goons left my sight, I wouldn't have left the diner. I'm not a big hero, Siara."

She looked at him. "You saved Jeremy."

Harry shrugged. "An accident. I didn't know what I was doing."

She frowned. "No. Part of you did."

Harry stopped short.

"What?" Siara said.

"I don't see them."

She peered into the dark. "They couldn't have gotten far. Let's go up a block. At least some of the streetlights are on."

He shook his head. "You don't understand. I don't see them *and* I'm not wigging out. I'm fine. The bad craziness is gone."

He inhaled and patted his chest, feeling fit.

"I say we just get the hell out of here," he said.

"But we came so far," Siara objected. "And we had a deal. You know, my poem?"

"Yeah, look how far we've come," he said. "This place is dangerous in the daytime."

She grabbed his jacket and pulled.

"Harry, people go through their whole lives begging for some kind of meaning, and you, you've just got it, can't you see? Something brought you here. It's like what your father was looking for and couldn't find. I'm not saying your dad would make the cover of *Good Father Monthly*, but look at what your brain's done. You see things no one else can. You can change them," Siara said. "Maybe it doesn't make all the hurting worthwhile, but if it's not worth *something*, then all you've got left is the pain."

Harry shook his head at every word. "Don't try to out-think me, Siara. That's my whole problem—too much thinking. My dad believed you could *think* your way out of anything, even death."

"Well . . . maybe in Todd's case, you can," she answered.

Harry clenched his hands into fists and slammed them into his thighs. "No!"

"Something drew you here. How can you just walk away?"

"Like this," he said. He whirled and started walking away. "We can call the cops and report some suspicious characters if that'll make you feel better about Todd, but I can't deal with this right now. It's been a *really* long day! I just want to go—"

The last word never came. He was staring at a thin space between buildings. On his right was the last of the town houses; on his left, a tall, grim structure that might have been a factory or warehouse once upon a time. Right in front of Harry was an alley, windswept, filled with trash. In center of the alley, floating maybe fifteen feet up in the dark air, was a pink balloon with a clown on it. It seemed to glow, like the moon.

"This is it," Harry whispered. He took a few steps in.

Siara followed. "This is what?"

"The alley from my visions," Harry said. "Where Todd falls and dies. This is it."

He turned toward Siara just in time to see the tallest member of the trio step out behind her.

"*Da*. This is it," the brown-haired man said.

His companions also stepped out, blocking any exit from the alley. The tall one kept his hands in his pockets, but each of his brothers flashed a long, sharp knife.

10. "Why you follow us?" the tall one said in a thick Russian accent.

His two brothers circled.

We're going to die, Siara thought. *They may even torture us first.*

She looked to Harry, hoping he might know what to do, but he just stood there, shaking. She wondered if he was having one of his A-Time fits. Either way, to these guys, he probably just looked weak and fun to attack.

"Why you follow us?" the tall one said again, slowly this time, as if they were the ones who might be having trouble with English.

Think, think, think, Siara! Make some kind of leap!

"We want to buy crack!" Siara blurted.

"We do?" Harry said.

"Yes," she said. "That's why we followed you. We just want some crack. So . . . do you have any . . . crack?"

"You don't look the type. Your boyfriend does, not you. You have money?" he asked.

She started fishing in her book bag. The tall one grabbed it and her hands shot up in surrender. "Just take it."

He nodded as he pulled the little purse free from the bag. "Spasiba." Siara thought he looked like a large rat, sniffing for food among garbage.

He paused from his rummaging to look up at them. "You dyaytee think you're so smart. We saw you all the time, so we led you here, where no one else sees."

"You're lying. You didn't see us. You're here to make a delivery."

Who was that? Harry?

She looked over to him again. His eyes were narrowed. He seemed annoyed, oblivious of the danger.

"Harry! Shut up!" Siara said. *Not a good time to contradict the drug dealer!*

The man raised a finger at Harry. "Listen to your girlfriend, Harry."

Harry said nothing, so the man went back to fishing through the purse, poking his long fingers through her property. He was visibly disappointed by the few bills he found.

The short, squat one stepped closer. "You are pretty," he said.

Suddenly Siara wished she didn't look so damn cute today.

"Yerik!" the tall one barked. At first she thought it was some Russian word; then she realized it was the short one's name. But Yerik didn't move. Instead he blew a kiss, giving her a good strong whiff of his disgusting breath.

"Get away from her," Harry said.

Oh, God . . .

Harry leapt between them, grabbing Yerik's arm.

The tall one whistled at Harry's bravado. "Shouldn't touch Yerik. He hates that."

Yerik kneed Harry in the crotch.

"You see?"

Siara made a small animal moan, as if she were the one getting hit. Harry, his face beet red, doubled over. His mouth opened, as if he were going to throw up, but a blow from Yerik's knobby fist sent him falling sideways. He hit the ground, rolled onto his side, and lay there gasping.

"You're going to kill him!" Siara shouted.

Yerik nodded.

Siara tensed, ready to dig her fingers into his eyes. A year ago, at her father's insistence, she'd taken a self-defense class, and all the quick, terrible things one could do to an attacker rushed grimly into her agitated mind. Not quite trusting the strength and sharpness of her nails, she grabbed the lid of a garbage can and pulled back to swing it at Yerik's head.

A knife at her throat stopped her. The last brother, the thin, skeletal one with the cap, had come up behind her.

"No," he said. "Just watch."

The flat metal of the blade felt icy against her skin. She couldn't tell if its edge had pierced her skin or not. Horrified, she gritted her teeth and did as she was told, watching Yerik kick Harry, first in the side, then in the back, harder and harder, like Harry was a stuck door that desperately needed to be opened.

For a while Harry twitched a bit. Then he stopped moving completely.

Dread coursed through her body ahead of the words. *He's dead! It's my fault! We should've left when he wanted to!*

"Aghh!" Siara screamed. She reached behind, stuck her fingernails into a patch of facial flesh, and ripped downward. The grip on the blade loosened. She slipped down and away.

"Andrei, you hurt?" the tall one said with brotherly concern.

Andrei hadn't cried out, but he was bent over, covering his eye and the side of his face with his hands. As Siara grabbed the garbage can lid again, she watched the tall one lift Andrei to standing and pull away the protective hand. Blood flowed from a deep scratch. She'd missed his eye by a fraction of an inch.

"You're fine," the tall man said, slapping Andrei lightly. "A scratch. Don't be a baby—you make me look bad."

Yerik stopped kicking Harry to see what all the fuss was about. He took a look at Andrei and shook his head. Then all three turned to Siara.

"You want crack? We'll give you crack."

They took slow steps toward her, making her move deeper into the alley, their worn sneakers scraping against unforgiving ground.

skrtch skrtch skrtch

She stepped back, matching her steps to theirs. She felt like a stupid little kid, playing at being a knight with her garbage can shield. She thought about the wild poet her teacher, Ms. Tarina, insisted lived in everyone, and wondered why hers was always on vacation, why her fear always seemed to overwhelm her passion.

Not knowing what else to do, she cried out, "Run, Harry! Run!"

But Harry was just a pile of clothes and flesh, not so different from the rest of the trash on the ground. Was he still alive? Had Yerik stabbed him? Harry's sparkling hazel eyes were gone. They'd rolled back up into his head. All she could see were the whites.

Like multicolored cake batter pouring sideways from a pan, the bodies of the three muggers dripped into long and winding trails, along with the rest of the world, until they just didn't look very important anymore. Even Harry's excruciating pain, which mere seconds ago had formed the center of his universe, vanished in a blur of sensation.

Harry was in A-Time. Siara's kiss was a nicer way to travel, but either the powerful blows from Yerik or his own panic had produced the same result.

"Siara," he said, planning to tell her about it.

Not here.

Which meant she was back there, in the alley with

the muggers, back in the sad little world of bits and pieces, where all things, even wonderful things like Siara, could suffer and die. Frustrated, grinding his teeth, he spun around, scanning the terrain, the flitting Timeflys.

Perfect! What good is this, what good is understanding, *if I can't help her? I'm just as pathetic and helpless here as I was in the alley! Maybe* more.

"Unk! Unk!"

The big bad Quirk was near Todd's trail, sniffing about, shivering cheerfully.

It looks like it's about to get what it wants. I guess that means Todd will be doing his swan dive soon. I'll die from a beating and Siara will be killed. That just about wraps things up for all the players in this *little mess. Thank you and good night, everybody! Hope you enjoyed the show!*

Looking down, he realized he was standing on Siara's trail. A rushing hiss of ebullition told him he was also near the event horizon. The future would soon pass.

It all tortured him, as if an answer were right there in front of him but he was too stupid to figure out what it was. All he had was knowledge, the ability to see the future, maybe change it, like he had for Jeremy—but that seemed like such a frail, fragile thing to use against a bunch of muggers. And there were no folding chairs around.

He heard a voice in the back of his head: *God does not play dice with the universe.* This time he recognized whose it was—his father's. The frightened man who'd lost a wife and turned his son into an expression of his rage against the universe machine.

Then there was Siara, saying, *You see things no one else can. You can change them. Maybe it doesn't make all the hurting worthwhile, but if it's not worth something, then all you've got left is the pain.*

Was it worth anything? Was he?

At least I can try. I can go see what comes next.

He moved forward, tentatively following Siara's trail as it bent toward the three other trails he assumed belonged to the Russian trio. His own trail wobbled nearby, but he was sure entering it wouldn't be possible. If Harry was going to see what would happen to Siara in the alley, he'd have to break his promise and eavesdrop on her life again.

I hope she'll still be around to hate me for it. . . .

He sprang ahead on the springy future until he reached a point where all four trails separated. With a shrug to whatever gods there were and an apology to Siara, he plunged into her future.

A scene rose quickly. Red and blue lights splattered across the walls of the alley he'd just left behind, making it look like a Hollywood crime scene. An ambulance and a police car were parked on the street. The brothers were gone. Todd Penderwhistle lay dead on the ground, head in a puddle, neck all bent and out of place. There was a second body, too, wrapped in one of those plastic things with the zipper he'd seen so many times in movies or on TV. What was it called? A *body bag*?

It felt like being in his father's hospital room all over again. He steeled himself and moved in for a closer look.

The bag was on a gurney, the zipper open just a little. Harry thought he'd see his own face lying inside there, but it was worse. Through the flap, he saw a strand of plum-red hair.

Siara!

Her tunnel ended, all black.

"No!" Harry screamed. "No!" He plunged his hands into the ghastly image, wanting only to destroy it. It wasn't solid. He couldn't feel it exactly, but there was pressure wherever he pushed, and things shifted around his hands.

He trembled and wondered, *What does that mean?*

It was soft like clay, malleable but connected, as if everything were one big piece of something. If he pressed on one spot, ripples raced in two directions— back to the past, where the ripple thinned, grayed, and stopped; and ahead into the short future, where it became wild and pulsating.

He pressed harder. The color of the body bag changed from black to brown. His mouth opened wide.

Did I do that?

He pressed even harder—a different driver was behind the wheel of the ambulance. Harder still and an entirely different ambulance crew was on the scene, and Siara's trail seemed a few feet longer.

I'm changing the future! Harry thought. *I can change the freaking future just by molding it!*

Ecstatic but terrified, he pulled himself up and out of the trail and looked around. The event horizon was coming. Everything he'd just seen would be happening soon, including Siara's death.

I've got to think! I've got to change things so Siara lives! Oh, God, thinking is, like, the only thing I can do well, and now I'm seizing up!

So, without thinking, really, he found the tall Russian's trail and dove into it, stumbling several steps into the future. The eldest brother (Harry now knew his name was Sergei) picked his nails while in the shadows, his brothers, Andrei and Yerik, did something unspeakable to Siara. Whatever it was, she couldn't even scream anymore.

Harry wobbled and flushed. He couldn't bring himself to look at her. Instead, realizing there wasn't much time, he plunged his hands into Sergei's face, hoping to somehow hurt him. The face warped beneath his fingers. Wherever Harry touched, lines of energy spread in either direction. Once the ripples settled down, Harry could see he had indeed had an effect.

Sergei had stopped picking his nails and joined in with his brothers.

Oh no, oh, God, I made it worse!

Panting, fearful tears welling in his eyes, Harry yanked himself out of the trail.

Sssssssssssssssssssssssssss! The event horizon edged closer.

This place is supposed to be timeless, Harry thought. *Why am I dealing with a freaking deadline?*

"Urk? Urk?"

The sound snapped Harry's head around. A small Quirk, no bigger than Harry's hand, was poking around Yerik's trail. Desperate, Harry scooped it up and wrapped his arms around it. It squirmed, trying to free itself, but before it could, Harry dove into Yerik's life, pulling the Quirk along with him.

The spot he entered was a few minutes earlier than the last. This time, Siara was standing in the alley, brandishing a garbage can lid, trying to look threatening.

Yerik stepped forward, grinning. She took a swipe at him. He easily avoided it. Just as it seemed he was about to grab the lid from her, Harry pressed the squirming Quirk into the trail. It vanished with a pop.

Yerik grimaced, grabbed his leg, and stumbled.

"What *is* it with you tonight, Yerik?" Sergei asked. "First the scratch, now you fall on your own feet!"

"Charley horse!" Yerik groaned, trying to rub the knot out of his muscle.

Harry smiled grimly. It was a charley horse Quirk, perfect luck. He shook off his sense of accomplishment and popped his head out of the trail. From what he could see in the near future, Siara's trail was a few yards longer. He'd delayed her death a few minutes, buying himself some time.

Think, think, think.

Interfering directly with the brothers was dangerous. He might leave Siara dead sooner rather than later. Maybe fooling around with other trails was a better bet?

Can I get the police to show up? What the hell would a policeman's trail look like?

Ahead, the lives of the three brothers veered off in unison, then joined with a fourth trail. Harry's intuition tingled. That fourth trail felt somehow significant. Looking back into the past, he noticed the brothers had hooked up with it earlier, probably *before* Harry had seen them in the diner.

What's that about? It's not Todd. Who is it?

Rather than guess, he bounded over and entered the mysterious trail. He soon found himself looking at a large, open apartment with thick carpeting, tall windows, and a gurgling fountain. There were wild paintings on the wall, a built-in aquarium, gaudy lamps, stainless steel kitchen cabinets, and painted walls and floors that even Harry could tell didn't match. It looked, *felt* like it had been put together by someone who had too much money and wasn't sure how to spend it. There was gold trim everywhere. Even the bling had bling.

A bald man was sprawled on a plush couch watching football on a plasma screen TV. Three cell phones sat on a glass end table, next to a bottle of scotch and several vials of white powder. As the man sipped the scotch, Harry could see that his teeth were capped in gold. The sip must have been particularly bitter, because he coughed and mumbled something in Russian.

Bingo. Sergei's boss. What can I do to bring him online?

Harry stuck his hand into one of the cell phones. Fingers of energy arced into the future. In seconds, the opening strains of "Who Are You?" by the Who played on the ringer.

The bald man grunted, muted his moaning TV, and grabbed the cell.

"What?" he said. "Pakaa? Gunning? Laadna, laadna. Sergei's doing a delivery there. I'll send him."

He pressed one button to hang up, another to dial.

Well, I did something.

Eager to learn what, Harry leapt out and raced back to Sergei's trail. He reached the alley just in time to hear the Russian's cell phone chirp. Yerik was still rubbing his leg; a fearful Siara still holding her garbage can lid.

"Hang on, Siara," Harry whispered.

"Yeah?" Sergei said into his open phone. He listened, then snapped the phone shut.

"We have to go," he said to his brothers. "Different delivery."

Andrei and Yerik looked at him.

"Saychaas," he commanded. "Now."

He tossed a backward glance at the terrified Siara.

"Lucky girl," he said. Then the three of them walked off.

Yes!

With a little tingle, the event horizon passed through Harry. The scene turned solid.

I did it! I saved her. I changed the future! I'm not a total loss, even if I really am crazy!

Millions of other thoughts about the world and himself crashed through his mind, knitting themselves into half-baked theories and blatant assumptions. For the first time in aeons, they all made him feel pretty good.

As Harry watched, Siara dropped her garbage can lid and ran toward a still form on the ground. Tears were in her eyes.

Who's that? Harry wondered. *Oh yeah, it's me. Ow! That looks like it's gonna hurt. So why can I see me here but not in my own life?*

As she started to roll him over, he felt a strong impulse to leave. Much as he wanted to see himself, as he had the first time he'd come to A-Time, the impulse grew too strong to ignore. He pulled himself out of the trail.

Maybe I was able to stay because I was unconscious?

He felt her hands on him, heard her voice start to pull him back.

No, not yet.

Fighting the desire to return, he searched for a certain dark and ugly life trail that had been plaguing his mind.

Mr. Todd Penderwhistle. Maybe I can end this all right now and change your future, too. It'd be an awful lot easier than trying to meet you.

Careful to keep hidden from the big Quirk, he slipped into Todd's trail, then raced over to the funny fork in Todd's life. Harry took a closer look at the wall, the section that was different from the rest of terrain, where the texture didn't quite fit. All around it were what looked like stitches, echoes. It occurred to him in a flash that they looked just like the little lines of energy he made when he stuck his hands into the future. Only here, the color had been drained.

I know *what this means.*

As he ran his fingers along the stitches, a weak part of the wall, the size of an egg, came free. Now there was a small hole and something beyond.

What's this? An alternate future?

He pulled at the hole's edges, as if unwrapping a present, revealing what had been buried. As soon as he saw it, his mouth dropped open.

I don't believe it. Todd? Is that you?

"Harry! Harry!" Siara shouted. She was getting frantic, probably thinking he was dead. He wanted to stay, to see more, but the pull was too strong. Like it or not, he was heading back to linear time, into a body that had been badly beaten.

Pain flooded him as he reentered. His left side, foot to head, felt like a rotted piece of fruit. His jaw ached. He was afraid to touch his teeth with his throbbing tongue, worried they'd be loose.

"Siara . . . Siara . . ." he moaned more than said.

He felt her dab at a sore spot on his face with a some kind of paper. It hurt.

"Shhh. It's just a napkin I found in my bag. Relax," she said. "It's okay now. They're gone."

"I know," he said. His bruised face bent into a smug smile, but that hurt too. "I did it. I changed the future. I sent them away."

She scanned his face. "You were in A-Time?"

He nodded. "Tell you all about it, but we've got to move fast. Todd's about to kill himself . . . and I think I know how to stop him."

11. Though his voice was garbled by a huge swelling on his cheek, Harry talked a mile a minute as he dragged a befuddled Siara out of the alley toward the front of the building. "You know how sometimes things can seem forced, like an awkward conversation with your parents or a really bad date?"

A yank at the front door revealed it was locked. Harry's hands went toward a side window.

"Well, I've had this feeling ever since I first figured out Todd was going to kill himself that it didn't feel right, that it felt forced," he continued.

As he pressed up on the window, the rotted wood splintered in his fingers, threatening to fall apart. "I didn't think much of it because, well, it's kind of distracting having everything around me changing shape and color."

He pushed at the window again, gently, hoping to slide

it open. A glass pane teetered, then flopped inside. Harry winced as the glass shattered loudly against the floor.

He put his arm through the newly formed hole and felt for the window latch. "But even after I got my bearings, I guess, I just didn't really care much about what happened to him." He turned to Siara, looking guilty. "I never *wanted* him to die. It's just . . . I mean, this isn't the debate team. Here I am on Gunning Road with the sun down, freshly mugged, and my hand inside an abandoned building, you know?"

Her face fanned into an odd mix of sympathy, affection, and bemusement. Harry felt like he was Pooh and she was Christopher Robin, about to call him a silly old bear. "You're not responsible for everything, Harry. I just had this silly romantic thought that we should try, and it almost got us killed. Todd's life—it's definitely not worth yours in exchange."

"I appreciate the thought," he said, still rummaging for a latch. "But I think you were right the first time. There are sins of commission and sins of omission. My father taught me that. He was really big on the whole 'sin' thing. Maybe I'm not responsible for *everything*, but when I see a broken future and know I can change it, it sure as hell feels like I should."

Harry hit something. He grunted as he pulled.

"Got it. Give me a hand. I don't want the whole window to break. I don't know who or what's in there, aside from Todd."

Together they pushed on either side of the wooden frame. Despite years of paint and rot, it slid along its track, leaving a gap a foot and a half high.

Harry climbed in. If it was dark outside, there were no words for the lack of light here. Something crunched and skittered as he hit the ground. He turned back to the window, wrapped his arms around Siara's, and pulled her in.

She slid from his arms to the concrete floor. The window glowed, allowing them to barely make out each other's faces.

"Point being, whenever I stuck my hands into the trails, it made these patterns that changed things. That's how I got rid of the Triage Trio, the muggers. Anyway, the patterns I made when I rearranged the trails were really bright at first, but even when they faded, you could still see them. It was like I'd left fingerprints."

"What's that got to do with feeling forced?" she asked.

At the sound of her voice, tiny feet skittered on the floor. A few shadows hurriedly slipped away.

"Rats," Harry whispered. "A bunch of them, too. Don't worry, couldn't be worse than a Quirk, right? Although they do apparently like to eat baby fingers. . . ."

He took her hand, rubbed it to warm her, then led her away from the window, into the black.

"Right before you snapped me out of A-Time, I was

in Todd's trail, at the spot where his life gets cut off." He tightened his grip on her hands. "I thought I was alone. I thought maybe I was the first to come to A-Time, but I was wrong, *really* wrong. There were fingerprints all *over* Todd's life. *Someone* changed it."

"There are other people in A-Time?" Siara said, her eyes widening. "It seemed so much like we were alone."

"Well, I'm assuming it's a person, but even if it's not, it's definitely something *intelligent*. Whoever it was made Todd's life more attractive to the Quirk. Someone *wants* him to commit suicide. It's not this weird sort of meta-natural event at all. It's more like attempted murder."

Plaster and glass crunched beneath their feet.

"But who would go all the way to A-Time just to get Todd to kill himself?" Siara said. "It doesn't make sense."

"No, I'm sure it does," Harry answered. "We just don't understand yet. It may not just be about Todd. It turns out his life is connected to certain other future events."

The hazy outlines of a steel-and-concrete staircase slowly appeared before them, right where he expected it. Lit by a few glowing windows, it rose up, story after story, to the full height of the building.

"In any case, thanks."

"Thanks? For what? What do you mean?"

"Well, like I said, if he just wants to kill himself, it's different, I think. Triage. If someone's trying to kill him, it's like Jeremy in study hall all over again. I can't just let him die. So, you were right. I really *do* have to save Todd."

She tugged at his arm. "Told you so."

Harry led her up the steps. "So what's your plan?" she asked.

He made a face. "That Quirk is too big for me, I'm not very good at arranging life trails, and there's not much, um, well, *time*, actually. The event horizon will pass over Todd's suicide soon. I was joking in the diner, but I'm hoping we can figure out some way to get Todd into A-Time so *he* can handle the Quirk. Sort of like Godzilla versus . . . well, Godzilla, really."

As they mounted the first few steps, the staircase wobbled and creaked. Siara shook and nearly stumbled, but Harry kept his balance.

He was getting used to the way the world moved around him.

Todd's open coat flopped easily on either side of him, like wings. He felt like he was in a western or *The Matrix*, headed out, all in black, to face down the ultimate great big badass, guns blazing, lights flashing, body smashing.

But the only thing he faced, really, was a big window.

Tired of waiting for his delivery, worried Sergei'd been picked up by the cops, he'd decided to just kill himself now, before he changed his mind.

At least maybe I can do this right.

His long leg stepped onto the sill and tested it. The old wood flexed but held. It was too thin for much more than the toe of his boots to fit on, so he had to reach out his arms and grab either side of the frame to pull himself up.

The handcuff dangled from his right hand. The wound on his left still bled freely.

So here I am.

And there he was, in the window. Not a normal apartment window; it was a tall warehouse window. It had seemed even taller when he lived here with his mother. Now, finally, it was a nice fit. He wondered what she'd think of it if she were still alive, if she'd won instead of lost that prison knife fight. No one at RAW even knew about it. Paperwork had probably gotten lost.

Damned if I was going to tell them.

Through the smoky glass he made out the low top of the building across the way and the alley below.

He pulled his hands, good and bad, away from the frame, reached to the bottom of the closed window, and pulled. The wood bent beneath him. It felt like the sill would snap before the window came up, so he shifted his weight and tried for a better grip on the frame with what remained of his bleeding left hand. The index, middle finger, and thumb held tight, but his feet almost slipped.

Shimmying his coat off his right shoulder, he covered

his good hand with the sleeve. Satisfied his hand was protected, he smashed his fist and arm into the glass and wood, lightly at first. Just testing. Then he snarled and swung in earnest, pivoting on the sill, swinging back so his blows would carry the full force of his weight.

The glass was thick, but he'd always been good at destroying things. The secret was in pretending. He pretended the window was Jeremy Gronson. He pretended it was his dead mother. He pretended it was the rat that bit off his fingers.

Wood splintered and glass flew, out and down. Night air braced his cheeks and nose. He kicked away the debris on the sill to clear his way to the ledge. When he was finished, there was nothing left to stop him.

A grin came to his face, a satisfied look of *Screw you, world!* The ground below wavered, welcoming him.

This is it!

Skreeeeek!

"Wha?"

Todd whirled as the door flew open. Two kids, a vaguely familiar boy and girl, stood in the doorway. He didn't have time to place them. His shifted weight had taken him off balance. He reached out to steady himself, but it was too late. The edge of the sill cracked under him. His large form tilted like a falling tree. His body twisted, trying to give itself a center of gravity somewhere above solid ground, but momentum carried him—not into the alley, but crashing uselessly back to the floor. Dust rose around him.

I really can't do anything right. How lame is that?

He sat there, legs out, back straight, the tails of his coat bundled awkwardly under his butt—and glared.

"This had better be good," he said.

"Um . . . well, hello there!" the boy said. "Did someone here want to chase the dragon?"

Todd shook his head. "Too late."

He sprang back to standing and headed back to the window.

"I've made other plans."

"Wait!" someone shrieked. It was either the girl or the boy's voice had jumped up an octave. It hurt his ears.

The alley loomed before him again, but before he could embrace it, small hands grasped his shoulder and waist, pulling him back inside.

"Don't do that! Don't!"

It was the girl screaming. What did she care?

They were both small. It'd be easy to carry them out with him. The cops would find them all together, dead. He moved his foot for leverage but was suddenly again off balance, falling flat on his back, his head slamming against the floor.

Now he was angry.

The boy and the girl scrambled to their knees, breathless.

"Don't want to do that," the boy said. "Quite a drop out there!"

"You could get yourself killed!" the girl added.

Todd half rose on his elbows, trying to orient himself. Sitting up, he was nearly as tall as they were on their knees.

The boy spoke nervously, like talking was a tic: "So Zodd, uh . . . God . . . I mean . . . Todd . . . like I said, we're . . . uh . . . here to deliver your stuff."

"That's right," the girl said cheerily. "Chasing the dragon."

Todd's face twisted. He felt like he was looking at talking mice.

"Nikolai sent *you*? You two?" Recognition lit his dull eyes. He knew the boy. "Harry Keller?"

He looked around, out a far window toward the front of the building, then out the still-open door. He expected the cops to come pouring in at any moment.

"Um . . . yeah . . ." Keller said. "Times have been tough since my old man died. Everybody has to make a living, right?"

"Didn't I say I was going to kill you?"

The girl piped in. "But you were really angry then, and we weren't bringing you anything, right?"

Todd whirled at her. "Who're you?"

She looked down quickly. "Siara. Siara Warner. We had study hall together, but with a couple hundred people in there, no reason you'd have noticed me. Um . . . good to meet you."

His gaze danced from face to face. He drew short, staccato breaths. He'd expected Sergei, but was it possible? Once he'd bought crack from a guy in coke-bottle glasses and a business suit. The guy kept it in a briefcase.

"Give me the name of Nikolai's supplier."

The girl, Serina, Sierra, her eyes went wide, but Keller answered: "Fat Lonnie."

That was right. Todd relaxed a little but still couldn't quite wrap his head around it. Why not? A good buzz would make the last leg of the trip a breeze, and hell, he could grab whatever they had, then kick the crap out of them if he wanted and save the money.

Ha! Save some money for what?

"Okay," he said, standing. "Show me what you've got."

Keller seemed confused. "Show you?"

"Yeah. Show me the stuff. The heroin."

"Oh. The stuff." Keller's eyes danced around in his skull, like his wires weren't connecting. "It's just . . ."

Siara, the girl, jumped in. "Nikolai knew, for you, for tonight, it had to be special. So he gave us something different. It's not at all like what you're used to."

"Yeah," Keller chimed in. "It's exactly the same, only better. Much better."

Todd smiled grimly. "Nikolai figured this was it, huh? Sure. I'm probably all over the papers."

"TV, too," Keller added.

Todd nodded. "TV. Nikolai's a good guy. Tell him I said so."

"Will do. I mean, hey, you gotta love Nikolai, right? He's the man."

"He's the Man?"

"No, no, no. Not the Man. *The* man," Keller corrected.

"Right," Todd said, nodding.

They all looked at each other. Todd gestured impatiently.

"Let's go, let's go. Give me the shit. I've got the money."

Keller shifted on his feet. "It's not just about the drug. You've got to be in the right state of mind."

"Right state of mind? I'm depressed. I want to kill myself. I just want to see some nice colors when I go," Todd said.

"Oh, you'll see colors," Siara said.

"Colors like you wouldn't believe," Keller added. "But there's a little ritual, you know? You have to sit down, relax, clear your head for it to work."

"I want to see the stuff now."

The girl fished in some kind of bag. It looked like it was full of textbooks.

"Of course. But it's not what you're used to, so don't expect it to look familiar."

She held up a small green pill.

Todd frowned. "That looks like a Tic Tac."

"It's not. Believe me, it's not," Harry said. "And we'll give it to you in a second, but first we've got to work on that little ritual. You've got to relax. A massage could help."

Todd reared. "You want to massage me?"

Keller quickly shook his head. "No, not *me*." He motioned toward the girl. "Siara. Siara will massage you."

Todd gave her a little smile, but she looked like she was staring at a toilet someone forgot to flush.

"Me?" she squeaked.

Keller grabbed her hands and pulled her forward. "Yes. Just a little . . . massage . . . No big deal. Something to help Todd relax and get in the right frame of mind so we can give him the green pill."

"Okay," she said, giving in to his gentle tug. "But he's got to keep his eyes closed."

"Of course," Keller said. "That's part of the ritual. Eyes closed. That will help him relax too. You'll close your eyes, won't you, Todd?"

Todd eyed Keller. If he tried anything, he could snap him in two. But a massage, eh? The girl was kind of nice. Could she be part of the going-away gift from Nikolai? Nikolai really was a good guy.

What the hell? I'm going to die anyway.

"Okay," Todd said.

"Okay," Harry said, looking at Siara.

"All right, all right," she said. She raised her hands and motioned her palms toward the floor. "Sit . . . sit . . ."

Todd backed up a bit, then sluggishly lowered his bulk, sweeping his coat back so it wouldn't bundle under him. The instant he hit the ground and his muscles no longer had to completely support him, he realized how exhausted he was. He sensed her come up behind him and caught a whiff of something sweet in her hair.

"Eyes," she said. He closed them, figuring, *Why the hell not?*

There was a pause and a few harsh whispers Todd couldn't make out. He was about to peek when he felt her hands press into his shoulders. They felt tiny, like nothing at first, but she pushed down with her weight on the heels of her hands and started kneading the muscle. Todd's head slumped forward and something in his neck cracked. His breathing slowed. A tingle ran from his spine to his fingertips.

It felt like heaven. No one had ever rubbed his shoulders before.

"Picture everything moving in time, ahead to the present, back to the past," Keller said.

"Do you have to talk?" Todd growled.

"Um . . . yes. Yes, I do," Keller said.

"Make it quick."

"Okay, okay. Quick. What would be quick? What would be really quick?" Keller said. He fell silent for a while, and again, there was only the blissful rubbing.

Todd heard three words that made him instantly tense: "Massage his hand."

The girl's hands froze. Todd froze.

"Siara," Keller said again. "Massage Todd's hand."

Todd felt ugly, like a dog lying in the middle of the street after a car had hit it, its guts spilling out all over the place. And no one wants to pet a dog when its guts are spilling out all over the place.

But she did.

Her soft hand was just above his own, flesh against flesh. She pressed gently, grazing her full fingers against what was left of his. The touch was shaky, but then her fingers wrapped around his, even though they were still bloody from the cuff, and gently squeezed. As her warm palm pressed against stub and exposed bone, he heard a sad sigh. At first he thought it was her, but the voice was too deep. He realized it was him. He had sighed.

Todd struggled against a rising, unfamiliar well of feelings. They bubbled through him, burning whatever they touched. A picture popped into his head, an old fountain he'd seen in a park or on a postcard. The stone it was made of was really old, cracked and chipping, the paint faded and peeling. Only the water was clean. It slooshed and sloshed from one chipped stone basin to another, demolishing the fountain as it went, making deeper cracks, making the whole thing crumble.

To clean the fountain, it had to be destroyed.

Keller started talking again, but Todd didn't have the strength to answer.

"That's where the rat bit you."

How does he know that?

"It happened a long time ago, but the rat didn't just bite your fingers; it bit *you*. And it never left. Your past is still here, and so is your future, like the window. It's all here, all with you at the same time. You just have to look to see it."

Todd heard the words, but other than the pain they brought, he couldn't make sense out of them. His head swam. He wanted to lean forward and wrap his whole sick body around the hand that held his—but he was frozen. A rat, big as a bear, bigger, stood between him and the hand, chewing and stinking. Todd felt helpless. Even in his great black coat, he was like a baby abandoned on the floor.

"Where have you been? Where are you going? What will you want tomorrow? The line, Todd, the difference between the two? It *isn't* real."

A tidal rush slammed him. Was it the stuff? Had they given him the stuff? Slipped that Tic Tac thing into his mouth or his arm? It felt like it. It was numbing, dizzying. Only it wasn't crack, or heroin, or K; it was him, his whole life. It was like his whole life had become a drug.

Todd's huge body slumped forward, but Siara kept hold of his hand until his eyes rattled and rolled up into his near-bald skull. Her disgust overcome, she slipped her hand out from his the way she might that of a sleeping child she'd been asked to babysit.

"Harry," she whispered. "I think he's gone."

No answer.

"Harry?"

He was standing but barely, his own eyes only showing whites as well. He was gone too. His body began to list dangerously to the side, and Siara raced over to catch him just in time to guide him to an awkward seated position. It was done. Harry was in A-Time with Todd.

And I'm here. Alone.

In the first true silence she'd experienced for hours, Siara wondered how worried her parents were, if they'd believed her phone message about a frightened friend. She thought about their conversation that morning, in their cozy little eat-in kitchen, about doctors and lawyers and careers and money. Then she looked around at where Todd had been born and where she now stood and marveled at how far she'd taken herself from her working-class home, which she loved, even if it did have just one computer.

Siara straightened herself, stepped back, and looked at the two boys, two alien species from different worlds, visiting a third together.

"Men." She shook her head. "They reach a timeless state of consciousness, and it's like I don't exist."

She whistled nervously in the near dark, stared at the creeping shadows all around, hugged herself for warmth, and waited.

12. The sublime intricate secrets of the timeless universe rolled out before them. The giddy future lines danced; the solid past vibrated with being. Quirks skittered about the terrain, eager to occur, while Timeflys swooped and fluttered in an intricate, transcendental dance, singing in myriad high-pitched tones.

Now the hard part, Harry Keller thought.

"What the hell is this?" Todd Penderwhistle said.

"Um . . . Welcome to A-Time!" Harry said, forcing a smile.

"What the hell are *you* doing here? Where's the girl?" Todd said. He wheeled about like a punch-drunk prizefighter, ready to clobber whatever moved. "A-what? Welcome to what?"

Maybe this wasn't such a good idea. It's like I've

locked myself in a cage with a tiger and now I have to teach it how to use a computer.

Todd whirled toward Harry. "*This* is the drug? The special high? You don't even really know Nikolai, do you?"

Recalling, from his fight with the Quirk, that he *could* feel pain in A-Time, Harry backed away slowly as he spoke. "I'm really, really sorry, Todd. Believe me, I was going to let you jump, I really was. I would have pushed you myself, but it wouldn't have been right. There's something I have to show you."

"Shut up. Where's the girl?" Todd said. He closed the distance between them with one step and poked Harry in the chest.

"Probably back in the warehouse," Harry answered.

"I want the girl," Todd said.

"Me too," Harry said. "Looks like we're both out of luck."

Todd shoved Harry. He sprawled backward and hit the ground, hard. Anywhere else, he might have rolled into a ball and waited to die, as he had in the alley with Sergei and his demented brothers. But this was A-Time, and he was feeling that bizarre rush of confidence again. He shot back to his feet, shouting.

"Look, Todd, you can stomp on me and beat the crap out of me and kill me, then maybe even bring me back to life just to kill me again, but how about you do something really different and *think* for second? I *knew* you could kill me! Siara knew too! We risked our lives to bring you here so I could explain something so important, it may make you want to . . . I dunno, maybe *not* have your skull bashed out on the concrete! Maybe so important, you might actually want to live!"

Hey! Harry thought. *I'm yelling at Todd Pender-whistle! Cool!*

Todd was apparently surprised too, because he didn't hit Harry. Instead he bristled a bit, then turned away.

"You . . . you set up those chairs in the auditorium just so I'd miss Gronson, didn't you?" he said.

Now it was Harry's turn to be surprised. Todd wasn't as dumb as he looked.

"Yeah. Exactly. I did."

"Why? Why'd you do that?"

"I didn't think he should die just because he told you to move your legs."

"He was being an asshole."

"Even so."

Harry blinked and waited as Todd scanned the sky's shifting colors.

"Do you think it hurts when you die?" Todd asked.

Harry wiped his mouth and looked down. His mind filled with an image of his father in the hospital, covered in burns.

"Yeah. I think it does."

Todd nodded.

Harry took a cautious half step closer. "So, you think you could give me a few minutes of your time?"

Todd blasted air through his nostrils. *Like a dragon,* Harry thought.

"Go," Todd said.

Harry was confused. "What? You mean, like, leave?"

"No. Go. Talk. Get started. Why'd you bring me here?"

Harry breathed a sigh of relief. "Okay, here in A-Time past, present, and future coexist. Someone messed with your future, so instead of you doing something really cool, this monster, a Quirk, jumps into your life and makes you kill yourself. I brought you here to help defeat the Quirk because it's really big and mean, and, well . . . so are you."

Todd stared at him dumbly. It was clear he wasn't following.

"Let's make it simpler. See the big fat tubes all over the place?" Harry said, pointing.

Some time passed.

"Come on, the place is nothing *but* big fat tubes!"

"Okay, yeah. I see them."

"Those're people's lives. One is yours. They move from the past to the future. That little line of fuzz is the event horizon, the moment when future becomes past."

Todd grunted. "Is it like a ride? Like a roller coaster?"

Harry rolled his eyes. "No. Not like a roller— Wait.

181

Okay, never mind, fine. Yes, *just* like a roller coaster, only, you know, one of those haunted-house roller coasters. You get in, you walk, you see your past, your present, and your future."

"Hmph," Todd said, looking around. He poked at the ground beneath him with his boot. "Got it."

"Now, see those big monster thingies, like spiders, only with teeth and one eye? They dive into people's life trails and make them do things. There's a really big one near *your* trail trying to make you kill yourself," Harry explained. "If you don't kill yourself, something very nice happens instead."

"Life trails," Todd said slowly. "Which one's mine?"

Harry pointed to the big ugly one. "That one, over there. The ugly . . . uh . . . the one that stands out. This would be much easier if you could see your own future, but you can't go into it. It sets up a feedback loop, kind of like when you put a microphone next to a speaker and you get that . . ."

Todd wasn't listening anymore. He walked up to his trail, punched a hole in the top, and hopped in.

"Hey!" Harry shouted, scrambling after him. "You're not supposed to be able to do that!"

He raced after him, diving into the hole Todd had made. It sealed as Harry tumbled in.

As Harry oriented himself, a scene from Todd's childhood played out. It was in the warehouse apartment. His mother was there; Todd was maybe six or seven. Two policemen and a social worker were trying to take the boy away, but they had a big fight on their hands. The fight wasn't with Todd's mother, as Harry would have expected. She, wan and sunken-eyed, stood idly by, sucking on a cigarette, as two full-grown men and one woman tried to wrestle a frantic and screaming Todd to the door.

Watching his younger self get kicked around did not sit well with the present-day Todd. He punched wildly at the scene. Again to Harry's surprise, Todd's blows weren't centered on the adults who held his biting, kicking younger self; they were aimed at his mother. And every time he hit, spiderwebs of energy crackled out into time and space. They faded quickly, but the blows kept coming, echoing the helpless cries of the six-year-old as he was dragged from the only, albeit horrible, home he'd ever known.

The tunnel rumbled with the energy.

"Knock it off! Knock it off!" Harry screamed. He grabbed Todd's arm.

"Get off me!" Todd grunted, tossing Harry into the social worker. Cascades of energy rippled through her face and bleach-blond hair.

"You can't just start smashing things!" Harry said, jumping back up. "You don't know what that stuff's connected to!"

But Todd was punching his mother again. Bits of terrain tumbled from the ceiling.

In for a penny, in for a pound, Harry figured, so he jumped on Todd's back. He wrapped his legs around the thick torso and both arms around the muscular neck. Todd reached back and tried to rip Harry off, but Harry held on tight.

"I'm going to kill you, Keller!"

"Fine, kill me! But listen first. You knew you had a crappy life before you agreed to this. I brought you here because you could make your life better!"

"Better how?"

Unable to lose Harry, Todd jumped backward, slamming him into the side of the wall. Harry was winded but still managed to hold on.

"Ow! Ow! Ow! It's hard to explain. It involves proteins and molecular structures. Crap, this is *all* hard to explain, don't you think? Since you're here, you *could* see it yourself!" Harry said. "Only you're a little too stuck in this particular moment. Try to remember the feelings that brought you here. That rush of all things all at once!"

"The what?"

"Okay, never mind. Try to remember the girl rubbing your shoulders!"

Todd slowed slightly.

Harry heard a muffled roar from above.

"What was that?" Todd asked.

Harry looked around, unable to place the sound. In the trail, young Todd, his arms and legs pinned, was carried out the door, his little body squirming like a big worm. His mother took another long drag, then slid the chain into place.

"Unk! Unk!"

"It's the quirk! It knows we're in here, probably from all your stomping around."

The pincers of a stick-like leg tore through the top of the tunnel, nearly stabbing Harry in the shoulder. He leapt out of the way.

They're not supposed to be able to do that! I thought they couldn't come into the tunnels in the past! Jeez! Everybody's breaking the rules today!

Another leg tore through; then the two worked together to widen the hole they'd made.

Harry jabbed a finger toward the future. "Just go. Go that way. It'll be faster than me explaining."

"What do I look for?" Todd asked.

Bracing himself against the sides of the tunnel, Harry started climbing out. "It involves chondroitin sulfate proteoglycans. . . . Oh, forget it! You'll know it when you see it. Can't miss it. Meanwhile, I've got to stop that quirk from attaching itself to your life, or you *will* jump, whether you want to or not."

Harry moved to pull himself out.

"Keller!"

"What?"

"Why're you doing this for me?"

Harry hesitated. How could he explain his father's

belief that all life had to make sense? Describe the visions that drove him? Or Siara's conviction that all this was somehow meant to be?

"I really don't know. Maybe because life is too beautiful for words, or there are too many words for beautiful. I forget which," he said. Then he climbed out, leaving a befuddled Todd behind.

No sooner did Harry breach the surface than the Quirk swatted him with three appendages. One hit his legs, another his stomach; the third raked his face. He twisted sideways from the triple blow, stumbled back, and held up his hands to protect his eyes.

"Unk!" the Quirk said victoriously. It went back to ripping a bigger hole in Todd's trail.

How can it do that? Harry wondered. *The past can't be changed, can it?*

There wasn't enough time to figure it out. The Quirk was breaking through. Weaponless, Harry kept his head low and butted its huge body with it. The Quirk didn't budge.

Changing strategy, he grabbed the digging appendages, dug his heels into the terrain, and pulled. That worked—the digging stopped. The appendages came free of the hole. Only then they lifted themselves up and into the air, taking Harry along with them.

It was like being on Todd's back, only worse. Harry went upside down as he clung to the limbs. The appendages curled, righted him, then pulled him toward the toothy mouth. The eye at the end of the stalk looked at Harry. Harry looked at the eye.

"I'm really sick of being afraid," Harry said.

"Unk," the eye said.

Harry felt himself tingle as the event horizon floated through them. As if worried, the eye swiveled to follow its progress. It stared back at Todd's trail and seemed to sense something wrong. Maybe Todd had reached his future.

With a pained "Unk!" the Quirk dropped Harry. He stumbled back to his feet just in time to see it barrel along Todd's trail, full out, on all four appendages, bursting past the moving event horizon. The eye found its spot in the terrain and pushed through. Its body flopped forward and shivered.

Harry knew what that shivering meant: the Quirk was about to happen. It'd all be over soon. Todd would be dead.

Thinking he did not want to disappoint his father, Siara, or the future itself, Harry ran, legs pumping, directly toward the shaking beast. Unfortunately, he had no idea what to do once he reached it.

Back in linear time, Todd Penderwhistle's rudderless body stiffened and stood. Startled, Siara put her hand to her chest.

"Phew, you scared me!" she said. Then she realized he was *still* scaring her. "What happened? Everything okay?"

Todd turned toward the window.

"Todd?" Siara asked.

She took a step closer to get a better look at his face. His eyes still showed the whites. It was easy enough to guess that this meant that his soul, or whatever, was still in A-Time. Something other than Todd was moving Todd's body toward the window. The Quirk?

"Todd!"

She boldly stepped in front of him, grabbed his shoulders, and shook, hoping to bring him back the way she had Harry. Todd was bigger, though. As he numbly took a step forward, he moved Siara as easily as the air.

His big foot rose and found a spot on what remained of the cracked sill.

Siara screeched, right into his ear: "Todd!"

Her own ears rang from the shout, but Todd didn't react. She looked around for something to trip him or hit him with. She thought about waking Harry, but there wasn't time. Todd's right hand, handcuff still dangling from it, grabbed the frame and pulled.

Siara dove for him. Though the sill strained from the additional weight and the wooden frame began to crack, she didn't budge him. He was seconds from tumbling.

The new crack along the frame gave her an idea. She pulled at it, trying to pry the wood and nails away from the brick wall. Their weight helped. Crimson with rust, little by little, the nails gave, inches at first, but enough to shift Todd's weight.

As he, zombie-like, corrected his balance, the tip of one of her fingernails snapped. She ignored it, dug her fingers into the space between mortar and wood, and tugged for all she was worth.

Harry skidded to a halt a few feet from the trembling Quirk. It was too big for him to move, too big for him to even attract its attention. Worse, as the sizzling sound over his shoulder told him, the event horizon was approaching.

The terrain around him rolled and rose in hills and valleys, sometimes forming weird promontories. Some trails—maybe those of things, not humans—rose in spiky patches.

Hoping to find something to use as a weapon, Harry bounced into the hard past toward a group of trails that rose perpendicularly. He wrapped his hands around one and when he pulled, a whole section of terrain came free, like a sapling uprooted from wet earth.

He wondered what the effect would be in linear time—if, in the back of a filling station, a crowbar or something had vanished and reappeared. Whatever it was, Harry held it sideways, like a bat, testing its weight. It was heavy—thin where he'd grabbed it, thick like a ball at the far end.

He headed back for the Quirk. As he grew near, he

yelled, hoping a surge of adrenaline would give him some extra strength.

"Ahhhhhhhhhhhh!"

The Quirk didn't move. It couldn't have cared less. Harry lifted the piece of terrain into the air and swung. He didn't aim for the body, which he knew was built like a tank, but for the slender bit of eye stalk that remained above the ground.

Wok!

The rounded end slammed into the stalk, scratching it, maybe cutting it. A gray-green ooze flowed freely from a deep wound. The blow also dragged the eye halfway out of its snug hole. It rolled up, showing first its white, then its black pupil, which was focused now, full of pain and rage, exclusively on Harry.

Harry pulled back to swing again, but as he did, he had a strong intuition that the Quirk wasn't going to give him enough time for a second blow.

Wok!

As Siara pulled, the crack widened and the window frame gave. With nothing supporting him, Todd fell backward, landing for the third time with a grand thud.

Now let's make sure you can't do that again!

She grabbed his right arm and spun him toward the radiator. Before he could pull away, she snapped the bloodied cuff around its thickest pipe, then stepped back.

Eyes still white, Todd jerked his arm. He grabbed

his right wrist with his left hand and pulled again. Flakes of rust flew from the pipe; a ghostly moan rose from his throat. He braced his feet against the radiator, kicked, and pulled some more. The radiator shook but held. He was trapped.

"Phew!" Siara said to no one in particular.

She wondered if maybe now that he *couldn't* get to the window, Todd's future would change in A-Time. Maybe *she* had saved him.

Harry Keller knew he'd been wrong about a couple of things. The problem was, he couldn't always see when he was right. He'd been wrong about getting hurt in A-Time. He'd been wrong about people being able to enter their own life trails. He'd even been wrong about Quirks being able to enter life trails.

But he *had* been right in thinking he wasn't the first person to enter A-Time. Nor were he and Todd the only ones there now. Through Harry's latest battle with the Quirk, he was being watched.

As the wounded eye of the Quirk stared at Harry and its four appendages readied to shred him, nearby, hidden from view by a labyrinthine mass of trail, the Initiate stood, glaring. When a Timefly came too close, he swatted it. The pretty thing fell to the ground, its delicate chime broken and fading. It twitched a little, like a wounded bird, as the Initiate ground it with a heavy heel. It shivered as it, and all its lovely, unique colors, vanished into the terrain.

The Initiate was not pleased. He had to do something quickly or his initiation would be destroyed. The Initiate was not patient, but he was not permitted to show it. He moved smoothly, graceful as a shadow, leaving not so much as a mark as he passed. When he found the right spot, the right moment in the right trail, his hands slipped into it seamlessly. They were graceful, with long fingers, like an artist's or a surgeon's—fingers that knew exactly what they wanted of this world, exactly how to make it happen.

That was why the Initiate had been chosen in the first place.

Where his fingers touched, flashes of light trilled through the terrain. These weren't awkward blasts like Harry Keller's childish, severe efforts. These were delicate, lovely, *elegant*.

As the Initiate watched his patterns change time, he thought, with satisfaction, that what he was creating was far prettier than any Timefly could ever be.

At the sound of footsteps reaching a landing, Siara turned from the handcuffed Todd. Someone was right outside the door. She hoped it was the police. She hoped it was over. She was just about to cry out, "Over here!" but then she realized they might take Harry away. She couldn't let anyone find him in his A-Time coma.

Maybe I can drag him into the next room? Let them find Todd alone?

As good a plan as any. She raced for Harry's comatose form, but before she reached it, three shadows appeared at the door. They did not belong to the police.

"Not so lucky, girl," Sergei said. He stepped in, followed by his two brothers.

Siara's throat ached from trying to wake Todd and Harry, but she screamed just the same.

13. As Todd stumbled through the life that had made him suicidal to begin with, he tried to focus but found that everything he saw hurt more now than it had when he'd lived it.

There was the time he'd cheated to get into RAW, no big deal. Not so easy, though, being reminded of growing up with his useless addict of a mother or the time when that damned rat had bitten off his fingers. Or when his pathetic mother had gone and died or all the other pointless moments in his stupid life. But none of those really got to him, really hit him hard in the gut the way one thing did.

It was the gunshot, the one he'd fired at Jeremy Gronson.

When he saw it again, he could feel the trigger tingle in his fingers. He felt the need, he felt the firecracker sound echo in his chest as he fired. But this time he felt the wrongness, the desperation, the shame, the guilt. Even though Gronson had asked for it. Even so.

This isn't like a roller-coaster ride at all.

Much as it hurt, it all made sense after that. By the

time he reached his suicidal leap, it made so much sense that even his ambivalence about dying was gone. He was disgusted he'd bothered coming here at all.

Keller said there was a choice. 'Can't miss it,' he said.

If there were, it would have to come out of the blue, and nothing in his life did that. It all reeked of inevitability, as though he were a rock rolling down a hill.

But Keller had said. Even so. Why place any faith in that mega-geek?

'Cause he was scared of me, hated me, but brought me here anyway . . .

Wait . . .

He felt his fall at the window, felt the wind, felt his jacket open, felt an awful thunk as he hit. The end.

He figured that was it, but then the images blurred; everything got dimmer, less definite. His dead body turned into a hearse, then a couch, then a bag of garbage that got all white and brittle and flew away in the wind.

As his impending death grew less distinct, something else grew brighter. He saw the girl, Siara, cuffing him to a radiator. And then there was . . . another trail?

It was half covered over, like someone had tried to hide it, but whatever lay beyond was glowing. Warm fingers of light poked through. It made his death in the alley all but fade to nothing.

Is this what Keller was talking about?

Todd stepped closer. Shapes started to form, but

suddenly the light dimmed again and threatened to flutter away. The alley was coming back. Something was happening. Everything was changing again. His death was growing strong.

"Please, don't uncuff him! You don't understand!" Siara said.

Sergei tugged at the cuffs, testing their strength. Satisfied he couldn't pull them off, he fished in his pocket.

Yerik was standing nearest Siara, leering at her with crazed eyes, licking his upper lip. Andrei was still by the door, acting like he was on lookout, but the building was obviously empty. When he shifted in the dim light, Siara made out, with some satisfaction, the thick scratch she'd left on his face.

"He'll try to kill himself! He'll jump out the window!" she pleaded, hoping it would make a difference.

Sergei shrugged. "I think you knocked him out to take his money, which, by the way, is really *our* money."

Siara took a step forward.

"Hold her," Sergei said.

Yerik pulled her hands behind her, pinning her wrists. Even in the chill, his rough hands were clammy.

The tall Russian knelt by Todd. He slapped Todd on the cheek, the way a doctor would. A bit of drool rolled from Todd's parted lips down to his chin.

Sergei turned to Siara, annoyed. "What did you knock him out with?"

Yerik tightened his grip and stuck his tongue in her ear.

Gluchhh! Siara thought.

"Answer my brother."

Nausea rose in her stomach.

"We didn't knock him out, I swear! Look at him! How would we have knocked him out?"

Sergei slapped Todd again, harder. "So, what? He's just tired? Sleepy? Like your boyfriend?"

He shook the sleeping giant. He pulled back an arm and punched Todd hard in the stomach. Todd's body heaved from the blow, but otherwise he didn't respond.

"Dead?" Andrei asked from the door.

Sergei put two fingers under Todd's nose. He shook his head. "Breathing."

He pulled a bent paper clip from his pocket and stuck the edge into the keyhole of the cuff connected to the radiator pipe.

"Don't!" Siara begged. "Please!"

Click.

The cuff came free. Sergei rose. He was about to speak when a leaden rustling caught his attention. Todd was moving. Head bobbing as if it were no longer quite connected to his body, Todd stood. He faced the window and stepped toward it.

"She was right!" Yerik said. Andrei stepped inside for a closer look.

"Please . . . stop him. . . . Please . . ." Siara said.

Sergei watched with his head tilted as Todd mounted the windowsill. As Yerik snorted, Siara yanked her hands free from his grip and raced for Todd. Sergei grabbed her around the waist.

"You don't understand! He has to live!"

"You're right. I don't understand. Explain it," Sergei said.

She hissed in frustration. "I don't understand either!"

Todd rose, full figure, into the frame.

Now what? Harry thought.

The area at the end of Todd's trail was shifting, growing blacker, its end becoming more pronounced. Harry and the Quirk both guessed what it meant—Todd was vulnerable again. The Quirk dived. The hole its eye had been in was still there, so it easily forced itself back into place.

Harry was right behind it, smacking it with his club-like chunk of terrain. The first blow glanced ineffectually off its side, but the second knocked two appendages out from under it. The eye popped back to the surface.

With the future just about to happen, the Quirk went utterly insane. Puffing and panting, it pushed Harry down by hitting him in the chest with its eye. It pressed the eye down on him and pulled its whole body up so that its full weight pinned him.

Next the appendages came, all four at once, poking, prodding, clicking, close enough to Harry's face that he could see just how razor sharp the pincers really were.

He swatted, kicked, pushed, and drove each one back time after time, until finally one, just one, got past his defenses with a lucky lunge.

"Unk!"

Pincers open and extended, the appendage tore through his jacket, through his shirt, through him, cutting and tearing as it went. Thin fingers of energy, just like those he'd made in the trails, rippled out at the site of the incision, wrapping around him like visible waves of pain. His arms and legs still moved, but they were feeble, useless.

As the leg twisted deep inside Harry's gut, the other three prodded the rest of him, then arched back in tandem, ready to dive in and shred him, now and forever.

"Unk!" the Quirk cried happily.

Siara couldn't believe it.

"There's two of them!" Andrei cried with sadistic delight.

At first the three brothers seemed disappointed to see Todd hesitate and waver at the brink of his fall. But when Harry rose, eyes likewise white, head likewise bobbing, and started shuffling toward the same window, they all broke out laughing.

"Harry! Wait!" Siara screamed. She struggled against

Sergei's arms as Harry pulled himself up into the frame next to the wavering Todd.

What the hell is going on in A-Time? she wondered.

There was so little space left that Harry had to wedge himself under Todd's shoulder. The two were awkwardly struggling over who'd get to jump first.

"A hundred dollars says Todd goes first! Two to one!" Yerik said.

"The little one will slip through! I bet for Harry! Go, Harry, go!" Sergei cheered. He loosened his grip on Siara as he reached for his wallet. Siara tried to pull away, but Yerik caught her. Andrei stepped up to help hold her back.

Harry and Todd's bodies stumbled back and forth on the ruptured sill. It was like a comedy where two characters wanted to go through the same door at the same time and neither was willing or able to let the other go first.

Yerik and Andrei held Siara, but barely, their eyes riveted on the excitement at the window. She reached down, pulled off one of her sneakers, and hurled it at Todd and Harry, hoping it might wake one up.

Her aim was better than she thought. The sneaker smacked Harry on the side of the head. He wobbled sideways into Todd and nearly slipped through an open space, out into the air.

"Aiiieee!" she screeched.

"No fair!" Yerik said. "She's cheating! I want even odds now!"

If only I were with Harry. If only I could get into A-Time on my own.

Against all reason, she tried to quiet her mind, to reach deep inside herself and remember what it was like to make the bizarre trip from one state of mind to another. She tried remembering what it looked like. She tried remembering what it felt like, what it tasted like. Any detail she couldn't remember, she tried imagining. She even tried shaking her head until everything got blurry and sweat broke out on her forehead.

But for all the mad-eyed poetry of her being, nothing, not a damn thing, worked.

Todd's life trail shrank around him. His alternate future was collapsing. Todd accepted that, but he wanted to at least see what he was missing. He stuck his hands into the small hole his alternate future had become and tried to pull his possibilities back apart.

As he did, something else pushed into his back. It was the drop at the window. He felt the chill wind of the alley. He felt Keller wobbling near him. The shrinking web of terrain was shoving him back, whole body, to his suicide.

Screw that!

Todd grunted and tore. Bits of trail came free in his hands but more grew back, faster. He stuck his arms deeper into the hole. He dug harder, yanking free bigger and bigger chunks. He pulled, scooped, and threw great clumps of terrain between his legs, like a dog digging a hole. Just when it seemed as hopeless as the rest of his life had been, he started making headway. Screaming, setting his full rage free, he kept going, finally making the hole bigger. Chunks of terrain fell into the image of the alley, drifting down to the pavement in pulpy clumps, like a sickly, timeless snow.

Finally the warm light poked through again, hitting Todd square in the face. He had to stop and squint. He couldn't make out anything; it was too bright. In the instant he paused, the hole started filling in again.

Fed up, he grabbed either side of the hole as if it were the window frame and thrust his head and torso inside. The shrinking trail sealed around him until only his feet dangled over the last part of his life.

Wedged into the tiny space, he opened his eyes. The warm light was everywhere now, filling his field of vision. Slowly his eyes adjusted, and he finally saw what Harry Keller had seen.

As understanding swept over Todd, his pained rage and his life force lost the slender distinction between them and became, for the first time, one.

Harry Keller didn't know where he was, linear time, A-Time, or someplace else entirely, but he was rapidly coming to the conclusion that it didn't matter much.

He heard a muffled "Unk! Unk!" He felt a stabbing pain in his side where the Quirk appendage pierced him. At the same time, he felt a wooden windowsill beneath his feet and a cool wind on his face that carried familiar city odors.

The clown balloon was here too, the uninvited guest, the clown monster, mocking him, not letting Harry turn away, even when that was all he wanted to do. It made everything a joke, as if the devil were a stand-up comic saying, "Stop me if you've heard this one before. . . ."

Only of course Harry *had* heard it before, like a billion times, and it was absolutely the worst joke in the world. His life, that was.

From the moment his mother had died, his father had insisted everything had to make sense. He could see his old man's face, telling him, again and again, that he, Harry, could be the one to figure it all out. He could see Siara, her face full of understanding, and maybe something else he was too afraid to name, telling him he was *destined* to save Todd.

It finally came together. His father had been right. Siara was right. Harry *was* meant to be here. His whole life had been for this moment. His whole life had been about saving Todd. But it was also about something else. It was also about letting himself, letting this stupid dream of himself as some kind of brilliant savior, die.

It had never made sense that he should still be alive when both his parents were dead. Every moment since the lightning bolt had killed his father had felt like borrowed time, as if he weren't quite here anymore anyway.

The rest of the connections were simple: his mother had died so that his father would be driven to force Harry to understand. His father had died to push Harry over the edge, into A-Time. Now Harry would die to save Todd so Todd could fulfill his destiny.

True or not, right or wrong, it all made sense. God's world made sense.

It just still sucked.

He didn't want to die, but he felt like a stubborn child refusing to do his chores or eat his vegetables. Just whining instead of doing what was good for him.

What the hell, then.

The thought of no pain filled him. Somewhere far away his feet were slipping off that windowsill.

14. Harry expected that the next thing he was going to feel would be his body slamming into the alley floor. He hoped it would be fast, not too painful, and braced himself for the end.

But when it didn't arrive, he opened his eyes. He was still in A-Time. The sharky teeth of the Quirk had been stopped, held in place by two pale pink things that had wedged themselves in on either side of its powerful jaws. They looked like hands, hands grabbing, hands pulling. Strong hands. One was whole, but the other had two fingers half missing.

It was Todd. Todd Penderwhistle was trying to change Harry's fate.

Turnabout is fair play, he figured.

Todd pulled, and all at once, Harry saw beyond the browns and grays of the big round Quirk body up into the A-Time sky, where Timeflys circled lazily.

Todd pulled again. The huge eye that had been pushing on his chest lifted, opened, then turned to see what was holding its jaws.

Though the eye no longer held him, Harry was still

pinned by the Quirk arm piercing his side like a spear. Todd kept pulling; he groaned beneath the thing's full weight, but he still managed to yank it higher into the air. First one, then two appendages lifted, but one remained, the one stuck in Harry.

"Keller!" Todd growled. "Get out of there! I can't hold it forever!"

Harry found words. "I can't. . . . It's stuck . . . in me!"

Todd roared and pulled again. Harry felt his whole body lift, pulled along with the Quirk's remaining leg.

"Do it!" Todd screamed.

Half off the ground, Harry tried to comply, but it felt like he would disembowel himself. Still, Harry pulled. Todd pulled. At last, the Quirk pulled too, trying to reclaim its arm, the better to fight off the new attacker.

It came loose with a sickly *crik!*

Todd and the Quirk fell backward. Harry, free, fell inches to the ground. The Quirk howled, ocher liquid oozing from a torn appendage. Todd let out a laugh, apparently shocked to have been successful at something for just the second time in his life.

Terrified to look at himself, Harry felt along his body with his hand. He touched the edge of the Quirk stub. Its better half was still buried inside him. Before he could think about pulling it out, it wriggled like a worm or a snake and crawled into his gut. The wound sealed itself, leaving only a perfect, bright red circle, like the open mouth of a clown. The piece of Quirk was in him now, part of him.

Harry raised his head in time to see the damaged Quirk flop off its back and stand shakily on its three good legs. At about the same time, Todd got back on his feet. The two squared off.

Todd growled.

The Quirk said, "Unk! Unk!"

Godzilla versus Godzilla.

They huffed and puffed and stared at each other.

Perhaps humbled by the loss of half a limb, the Quirk slowly extended its eye and sniffed at the grim-faced Todd. It seemed to be saying, "Don't I know you?"

Todd growled again. The Quirk seemed hurt. It averted its eye and scanned Todd's life trail. When it could no longer find the spot it had dug for itself or any spot that might suit it at all, it shivered, terribly upset. Now it needed different food.

Harry sat upright on the terrain, his wound throbbing. The thing inside him started pulsing, pulling—drawing the Quirk. The Quirk raised its eye and came scrambling toward him.

It either wants its arm back or it wants me now instead of Todd!

Harry was too weak to move, but before the Quirk could reach him, Todd grabbed its eye stalk, digging his hand into the spot where Harry had already hurt it, hurting it even more. It pulled its eye back and snapped its teeth, more out of reflex than a planned attack. Todd ducked easily. Finally, with a longing look at Harry, the Quirk limped off, maybe looking for more accommodating terrain.

Slapping his hands together, Todd strode up.

"Keller, what I saw . . . it was amazing," he said. His voice sounded strange, different than normal. Almost awed.

"So then you forgive us for tricking you about the heroin?" Harry said weakly.

Todd grinned. "Yeah, I guess."

It was weird to see Todd grin—more disconcerting than comforting. Todd kept talking about how amazing his future was, but the pain in Harry's side started taking all his attention.

"Harry? Harry?" someone called.

Was it Todd? No. Todd was still talking about how surprising life could be.

"Harry? Come on, Harry!"

It was Siara. He wanted to answer but couldn't. The pain was deadening. It was telling him he didn't *deserve* to answer, that he didn't deserve *anything*. And it was getting louder and louder and louder until finally he couldn't hear Siara at all anymore.

A clown balloon winked and hovered. Then it flew away.

Siara nearly collapsed with relief as Todd's eyes rolled back into view.

"Todd!" Siara shouted, pointing. "Get Harry!"

Noticing that Harry was still next to him on the sill, Todd shoved him back inside, where he tumbled to the floor, unconscious. Todd leapt down, his weight raising a dust cloud. The handcuff still wrapped around his good hand clinked lightly. He looked around and quickly assessed the scene.

"Let go of the girl, Sergei," Todd said.

Sergei said something gruff in Russian but complied. Andrei and Yerik moved aside, leaving Siara free to rush toward the fallen Harry. She called his name over and over again, but to no avail. Harry wasn't waking up.

Todd pulled a wad of bills from his pocket and thrust it toward Sergei. The Russian took the money and handed back a small envelope of powder.

"Now get going," Todd said.

Sergei eyed Todd, then looked at the money in his hands. He spoke nonchalantly as he slowly counted the bills. When he finished, his blue eyes twinkled. "*Da.* We'll be going."

"Can we keep the girl?" Yerik asked.

"No," Todd said.

Sergei slapped his brother on the back of his head. "Don't be rude. This is business. We will buy you another."

Siara rose from Harry's side, fuming. She was ready to do something drastic to them until Todd said softly,

"They're the ones I bought the gun from. They're always packing. Let 'em go."

So she did. She let the three brothers who'd almost killed her and Harry twice just vanish out the door. Their footsteps and brash laughter echoed on the steps on the long way down. Maybe the world *didn't* make sense.

Todd looked at the envelope in his hand, made a face, and shoved it in his pocket. Rubbing the wrist that still had the cuff on it, he nodded gruffly toward Harry.

"Why isn't Keller awake? Is he still in that A-Time place?"

Siara knelt and cradled Harry's head in her lap, then gently pulled on his closed eyelids. The white still showed.

Siara said, "It looks that way. What happened with that thing, the Quirk?"

"I chased it away. It's not coming back," Todd said. He walked over to the window and looked outside. "It was pretty freaky. My future, I mean. If anyone had just told me about it, I wouldn't have given a damn, but when I *saw* it, when I saw all those lives, all those little flashes fanning out from my life . . . I mean, it's got nothing to do with who I am or what I am. More like I happen to be the right guy at the right time in the right place. But I'll take it. It's cool."

Siara shook a lock of dyed plum hair out of her eyes. "So, what is the great and wonderful thing you do?"

He turned to her with the strangest smirk. It made him look like a boy, despite the way he towered over her. "I'm not even sure I understand. There's this truck about to hit this woman and she's too busy staring at it to move, so I shove her out of the way. Then she goes and cures something, and a whole bunch of people, millions, get better."

He looked back outside. "You ever try and imagine what a million lives look like? I don't have to. I just know."

"What does it look like?"

"Like they're not separate people anymore. Like they're part of this big thing, bigger and better than each of them. Bigger and better than me, anyway."

A weak voice caused them both to turn. "There are these proteins in the human body," Harry said as he struggled to a seated position. "Chondroitin sulfate proteoglycans—CSPGs. They stop damaged nerves from growing back after an injury, like when Christopher Reeve fell from his horse. A woman who studies them will be walking across the street and she'll see a logo on a truck with a twisted loop that reminds her of the shape of the proteins. It gives her an idea about how to deactivate them, and it works. Kind of the same way Kekule, a nineteenth-century scientist, dreamed about a snake biting its own tail and came up with the molecular structure of the benzene molecule. That little flash of intuition would've been her last thought, but Todd pushes her out of the way and—ta da. A lot of people can walk again."

Todd jutted a thumb at Harry. "What he said. And it looked really, really cool."

Siara leaned down to help Harry up. "That's amazing, Harry. But are you okay? You were gone for a while after Todd came back."

Harry pushed Siara's arms out of the way. He scrambled to his feet.

"I'm fine," he said. He pulled away from her, lifted his shirt, and stared at his stomach as if expecting to see something.

"You did it," she said.

"Yeah, I know," he said, rubbing his side.

Siara moved beside him. "Harry, what's wrong? What's the matter?"

He staggered across the room. He held his hand out to stop her from following.

He looked at her a second, then averted his eyes. His head twitched back and forth. He played with some broken glass on the floor with his foot.

"So I guess I owe you a poem, huh?" she said, hoping for a positive response. She didn't get one.

"Look, Siara, I know you were expecting a big happy ending because you got me to save Todd, but this isn't *A Christmas Carol*, or *It's a Wonderful Life*, or even *Back to the Future*, so I'm not going to rush out and buy everyone a turkey," Harry said.

Siara narrowed her eyes, confused. "That's okay, I don't like turkey. Too dry. What's this about, Harry?"

"We're not all heroes now. We're not all fixed."

"What are you talking about? Did something happen to you?" Siara said.

"Now . . ." Harry said, shifting his head back and forth as if he were stoned, "I'm going to leave. You'll go as far as the stairwell and say my name four times, but you won't follow without your sneaker. By the time you find it, I'll be long gone. You'll look for me, fail, and Todd will get you a taxi home. You'll be worried, but you'll get over it. In fact, you'll be over me by Monday. Fifth period."

She stepped closer and tried to put her hand on his shoulder. "What is going on?"

He twisted away. "It'll be faster and easier for you if you just stop worrying now, okay? You won't because that's who you are, but you should know it'll be faster and easier if you do."

He hadn't looked at her the whole time. Without looking at her still, he all but ran out of the room.

"Harry! Harry!" she called, rushing after him.

She entered the dark hallway, nearly tripping on the way. He was on the stairs, taking them two at a time. It was dark, but she started to follow, until she realized her foot felt cold and damp. One of her shoes was missing. She'd thrown it to try to save Harry's life.

"Harry!" Her voice echoed down the stairs. "Harry!"

That makes four, she realized, annoyed.

His footsteps grew quieter and quieter.

She didn't know whether to be angry or not. She didn't know whether to be worried or not. She didn't know whether to be hurt or not.

But she was all three.

Todd appeared by her side and looked down into the stairwell's gloom. "Maybe you should leave him alone," he said.

She looked at him. "You mean the way we left *you* alone?"

Todd said nothing.

"Could you help me get my shoe?" she asked, pointing to her sock-covered foot. The sock was the thin kind too, mostly decorative. Her foot was freezing.

Todd nodded. The unlikely companions made their way to the alley, where they found her sneaker in a puddle.

"Funny," Todd said.

"Not to me," Siara answered, wincing as she forced her foot into its cold, wet confines.

"No," he explained. "That puddle's where my head would have been."

Siara looked out into the dark. "You don't think he'll hurt himself, do you?"

Todd shook his head. "No. He just looked tired. Fed up, maybe."

"What about the Quirk?" she asked. "It almost made both of you jump. Could it be after him?"

"I told you. It's gone."

She nodded, almost convinced. Then she turned to him again.

"Help me find him," she said. They walked out of the alley, Siara's foot going *squish squish squish*.

They spent two hours combing broken buildings and trash-strewn lots. There was even less light now than when she and Harry had arrived on their strange adventure.

Ours, she thought. *It was* ours, *wasn't it?*

Stupid thoughts raced through her head, like, *Was it something I said?*

Maybe Todd was right. Maybe Harry Keller had just been through enough for one night. No one on Gunning Street would ever be found unless they wanted to be, and it was clear, for whatever reason, that Harry didn't want to be found.

A few blocks later, a deep ruby, the color of diseased gums, appeared at the tops of the old buildings. It was dawn. When Siara complained about her aching feet for the sixth time in as many minutes, Todd said, "Maybe I should get you that cab."

Watching from behind some garbage cans, Harry felt like a grounded gargoyle, heavy, wind-worn, and flightless. The pain in his side had either subsided or he was getting used to it, but that hadn't helped his mood. He sighed as Siara climbed into the taxi.

In A-Time, with his wound making him feel lonely, desolate, and undeserving, something had driven him to peek yet again inside Siara's life. He was looking for confirmation, for reassurance. He still couldn't see his own future, but he was hungry to know what would happen to him, to them. So, feeling almost like a junkie now, he broke his promise yet again.

At first the trip had just been frustrating. Every time Harry and Siara were together, Harry felt forced to leave the trail. How had Todd done it? Was it because Harry was the seed, the thing that had brought him there? Or was Todd just stronger?

As in Todd's life, there were other possibilities, other choices—and in one, Harry wasn't part of Siara's life at all. So he followed that path, curious to see what might have gone wrong between them. There, he saw it—Siara kissing Jeremy Gronson.

And she liked it, a lot. Her parents were pleased too.

It wasn't fated to be; it was just a possibility, an image, Harry told himself, but it stung as badly as the Quirk wound in his side. Despair washed over him, threatening to drown him.

He knew she was better off without him, better off not running around after midnight with a loon, almost getting herself killed. And Siara herself had said he was no Jeremy Gronson.

So he decided to make it easier for her—to leave and

make sure her future was safe—without him. Maybe in a month or so he could explain it to her, explain what it had been like seeing her hair flop out from a body bag, explain how he felt gutted and unsure about everything, explain how lucky she'd be to stay away. But he couldn't just now because it hurt too much, because he was having trouble making sentences again. Because things swam in and out of focus, and voices flooded his head.

He would tell her just as soon as his heart stopped pounding, just as soon as he shook himself free of this funny urge to climb up to the very top of the nearest building and jump.

Harry Keller had started the day terrified that he was crazy, but since then he'd made an amazing trip, saved some lives, and even thought he had a real chance with Siara for an hour or so there, but now all the good felt like some freak accident, and he was ending the same way he'd started.

15. "We were worried *sick*!" Siara's mother said, near tears. "There was a *shooting*! Where *were* you?"

Siara had hoped she could sneak in, but her wild-eyed, sleepless parents were standing at the door.

"I thought you were learning responsibility," Papa Warner growled.

"I am!" Siara shouted. "I'm sorry! I just . . . I just . . ."

"Do you know that a *detective* called us?" her mother said.

"You're grounded for two weeks," her father commanded.

"Two weeks? If you're so worried about me, I'd think you'd just be happy I'm alive!"

Her mother folded her arms, sealing the deal. "You're lucky it's not four! Now, you tell us exactly where you were!"

Siara shook, shivered, then screamed, *"Because I could not stop for death, he kindly stopped for me!"* quoting one of her favorite Emily Dickinson poems.

"Are you on drugs?"

She ran to her room and slammed the door.

A few hours later, her father, pretending to be calm, knocked, came into her room, sat on her bed, and again asked what had happened. When Siara remained silent, he got angry, and when he was angry, he was less than delicate.

"You know, leaving that police interview could go on your record. How's that gonna look when you apply to law school?" he said in his can't-you-see-how-much-sense-I'm-making? tone.

Tired and drained herself, Siara had had enough of the whole being-these-people's-child thing. "I don't want to *go* to law school! I want to be a writer!"

He frowned, shaking his head, then turned and left.

She woke around noon, snug in bed. Despite the fight with her parents, she was giddy at having survived and feeling supremely conscious. Maybe it was just a holdover from her A-Time visit, but the same old books, stuffed toys, posters, and whatnot all glowed. Even the dust was intriguing. The mad-eyed poet inside her was ready to explode.

Recalling her deal with Harry, she finished her poem. Then she worked on three others just for the hell of it. When that rush wore off, she had to see him, to show him.

Ignoring the terms of her punishment, she escaped via the fire escape, risking even more trouble with her parents. She took a bus to Harry's neighborhood and knocked at his graffiti-covered door.

Then she knocked again.

And again.

Nothing.

"Go away," he finally yelled through the door. "You'll forget about me soon, I promise. Monday. Fifth period. Just wait."

I really want to see you, she thought, but she said, "Look, I came here even though I was grounded, after a huge fight with my parents, just to find out if you were okay, so please, just tell me if you're okay."

The door creaked open. Harry's face, unbrushed hair dangling in his eyes, appeared. He was nervous, more so than usual.

"See? Okay?"

"No, not okay. Why won't you talk to me?" she said. "We've been through this amazing thing together and I need to talk to you about it. Don't you need to talk to someone? I'd . . . I'd even talk to Todd at this point, if I knew where he was. Can't you just let me in?"

He shook his head and closed the door.

She waited a while, banging over and over, but he never came back.

As she left, Siara decided two things. The first was that Harry wasn't going to commit suicide. The second was that he was a jerk.

By Sunday morning the world seemed just a little duller, a little more annoyingly familiar. Colors faded, sounds grated. She did the whole apology song-and-dance deal with her parents, assured them that no drugs had been involved, and accepted her grounding without fighting. They stopped harassing her about the poetry class and said they just wanted her to be happy.

Happy.

By the time she arrived at school on Monday, everything was dead and dull again. Once again, the clock would not cooperate. Time, rather than running or warping or dancing, simply passed, all the way to the end of third period. Even so, she decided she would not abandon poetry, not just yet.

And Harry Keller she would give one last try.

Siara and her friends were supposed to walk to the lunchroom together, but she steered them by the auditorium, where she hoped he would be.

"So, after school, we're going to the pet store," Hutch said. "They just got a new shipment of puppies and we thought we'd all go squeal at them. Want to come with?"

"Can't." Siara sighed.

Hutch lowered her big round glasses and pretended to pout. "Come on. If you like, we'll make sounds only dogs can hear."

"I'm grounded. It's a long story, but . . ."

Before she could even think of a lie, Siara felt a hard nudge from Jasmine. "Did you *see* the way he was checking you out?" she said, her eyes bugging.

"What? Who?" Siara whirled. Harry? No. He was nowhere to be seen. Just the usual collection of bobbing heads and shuffling feet.

"Who?!" Jasmine repeated, chuckling with fake shock. "Jeremy Gronson! He smiled right at you, like the prince seeing Cinderella at the ball, and you didn't even look up!"

"Here I thought he only dated the vacant Barbie-doll type. What was Jeremy's last girlfriend's name?" Hutch asked.

"Barbie," Jasmine said.

"Really?" Hutch asked, grinning.

"Really," Jasmine confirmed.

Hutch started fishing in her bag. "Where's my PDA? I've got to IM Dree. She's got that icky flu, but she can drag her ass out of bed for a flirty Gronson sighting."

"Jeremy Gronson?" Siara said, finally hearing the name. "Flirty? Why would he look at me?"

"Uh . . . gee," Jasmine said. "Maybe it's the fact that you're adorable. And that outfit doesn't hurt, I'm sure."

"This?" Siara said, looking down at herself. She had on a corduroy miniskirt with a scoop-neck top and knee-high boots. "I barely even paid attention to what I wore this morning. . . ."

"Are you, like, in another dimension today?" Jasmine said.

"Not another dimension," Siara mumbled. "Just my own, only without linear time . . ."

As they came to the doors of the auditorium, she navigated them to a halt.

"What are you doing?" Jasmine asked.

Hutch watched her curiously. "Okay, Jazz, leave her alone. We're all still a little weirded out by the whole shooting thing, right, Siara?"

"Yeah. That's it," she answered. "Definitely weirded out." She scanned the auditorium.

Jasmine leaned back against the ceramic-tiled wall and held her books against her chest. "Do you believe Todd Penderwhistle turned himself in? What's that about?"

"Inbreeding, maybe," Hutch offered.

An electronic chime drew Jasmine's attention to her PDA. She spoke as she read, eyes widening into nearly perfect circles.

"Get this! Dree says there's a rumor going around that Siara and—omigod—*Harry Keller* were seen in a diner on Friday! Better squelch that one, fast."

Hutch kept eyeing Siara. Siara looked down and stared at the shine on her knee-high boots.

"We *can* squelch that one, right?" Hutch said. "You never did tell me where you rushed off to on Friday."

"Siara?" Jasmine asked. "Please don't tell me you're dating Harry Keller! I mean, I love you, but that guy is insane."

"He's not insane," Siara said sharply.

Jasmine's eyebrows shot up. "Oh my God, you *are* going out with that weirdo, aren't you?"

Siara rolled her eyes. "We're not dating. I'm not even sure we're speaking."

"Great relationship," Hutch said. "Nice strong boundaries, mutual respect. None of those pesky conversations . . ."

"So what is the deal, then?" Jasmine asked, her face full of confusion. "Because you seem mighty touchy about the guy . . . We're talking Harry *Keller*, right? The burnout?"

"I don't want to defend him right now," Siara said with a sigh. "I'm too busy thinking he's a jerk, okay? We had a little . . . something, I don't know, a date, a very, very long date, and I just wanted to see if he showed up here so I could make sure he was all right, you know? He's a little . . . damaged."

"A little? Like Hoover is a little dam," Hutch said.

Before she could think of a response, Siara caught a glimpse of wavy chestnut hair ahead in the hall. Harry Keller was slouching toward the auditorium.

"Harry!" Siara called. If he heard, he didn't react and soon disappeared inside.

"True love calls," Jasmine said, her voice dripping with concern.

Siara went fishing in her book bag, quickly putting her hand on the spiral-bound notebook she'd held when their paths had crossed on Friday.

My poem. We had a deal. Maybe at least he'll take a look at it.

"What's that? Weren't you quitting poetry class, like, on Friday?" Hutch said. "Is there no end to the mystery that is you?"

"Okay, so it's not stupid," Siara said. "It may be my life's calling."

"Siara, we're your friends and you're really starting to worry us . . ." Jasmine said.

"I know, I know. And I love you both, but could you guys just leave me alone for a little bit? I'll catch up with you in the lunchroom in five seconds and tell you everything, I swear!" Siara said.

At least, I'll tell you as much as I think you'll believe.

They looked at Siara, then at each other. Hutch pulled her bag over her shoulder. They walked off.

Siara glanced over the poem. She wanted to change it, but it was done. The thing she liked most about it was that she hadn't really done it for class or even for Harry. She was dying to show it to him, though.

Exhaling, she walked into the auditorium, growing more nervous with each step. Harry sat in an aisle seat, leg out, head buried in a book.

She walked up. Sick of saying, "Harry! Harry!" she reached out to touch him on the shoulder. Before her hand could make contact, he turned to face her.

"You have to leave me alone," he said.

"Can't you just look at my poem? You know, my half of our deal?"

He shook his head, then turned his back.

Siara was mortified. She had opened herself to the pariah Harry Keller, believed in him, believed in his madness enough to finally let loose her own wild-eyed poet, with all the fear and danger that entailed, and what did she get for it?

Fine. Screw this. Screw everything. Screw you, Harry Keller!

At long last she had a single word for someone, and it was *asshole*.

She tossed her spiral-bound notebook to the floor in front of him and stormed off. It landed with a splat at his feet. The page with the rest of her poem jutted out into the air, half folded.

For a while, Harry ignored the book, the same way he'd ignored her pleas. But once he was sure she was out of earshot, he looked up. As he watched her go, without looking at the page, he recited the poem word for word:

Simple crystal wishes
Open, pinprick sky
Losing track of all the little lifetimes going by
I lie on quiet island

But I'm hungry for the morning
And I'm hungry for the night

And I'm hungry for the taste of things
That hunger, live, and die

So knowing, growing, up goes the sail
Fighting through the tempests that the dreamy wind
  inhales
I head home from quiet island
And the clock on the wall said, *Tick. Tick. Tick.*

Epilogue

"Urnk! Urnk!"

"Tsk-tsk."

The mutilated Quirk nuzzled the Initiate. A long-fingered hand stroked the jagged tear in its appendage.

The Quirk whimpered.

The Initiate scooped a bit of soft terrain from the future ground, and patted it gently onto the wound. The oozing stopped.

"Irgggukkk." The Quirk sighed.

"My bad. I underestimated him. But I'll fix it. You'll see."

Understanding or not, the Quirk trundled off to sniff along the trails.

The Initiate, the only human shape visible in the weirdling landscape, once again made ready to do what he did best. He strode with long, even steps until he reached one particular, peculiar life trail, one that was uniquely full of twists and turns. The sloppy life was shaky to begin with: Keller was obviously suicidal, and he'd always seemed ripe, ready to collapse. Why hadn't he, then? Who could ever have expected such trouble from such a weak and fractured thing? Why hadn't the piece of Quirk already finished him off? What on earth still held this patchwork boy together? What gave the bug the strength to hold on?

The Initiate scanned the trail for an answer. He thought on all the lessons he'd learned about the time streams and tried to find something in his view that matched his question.

Ah.

It was easy to see. In the recent past, a second trail joined up with Keller's. It was cleaner, steadier, and whenever the two touched, Keller was lifted. Siara Warner steadied him.

I don't face a single opponent; I face two.

But the troublesome trails were separating already. Keller, in despair from his wound, was pushing her away.

How can I help?

The fingers of both hands pushed, long and full of feeling, into the lives of Harry Keller and Siara Warner. Deep purple pulses flowed blood-like through their futures. The trails seemed to fight the changes being made. They fought to remain intertwined, but the pulses kept coming, thicker, stronger, and faster, until, with a shudder, the two trails split completely apart.

With great satisfaction, the Initiate watched as Harry Keller's future grew more twisted and chaotic until, all alone, it came crashing to a halt.

In the distance, the wounded Quirk's eye shot up,

smelling a new opening for itself, an even better one than Todd's life had provided.

The hands withdrew. The Initiate moved on, satisfied that Harry Keller would be dead within a month.

Acknowledgments

A deep and humble bow to Liesa Abrams for having the exquisite taste to bring Timetripper into the Razorbill line and the patience to listen to the hundreds of potential titles I ran by her for this book. I've yet to work with a sharper, faster, or more understanding book editor than she. A similar bow to my incredibly hardworking and attentive agent, Amy Stout of the Lori Perkins Agency, for many, many things.

I am also indebted to the talented and keen-eyed writers comprising the Who Wants Cake crit group in NYC (Dan Braum, Nick Kaufmann, Sarah Langan, K.Z. Perry and Lee Thomas) as well as my ever-loyal first readers, Steve Holtz and Lesley Logan, the only two people on the planet who've probably read all my stuff.

It feels more serendipitous than ironic to have this, my first original published novel, based on my first original published comic book, so my heartfelt thanks also to Ken F. Levin and the folks at First Publishing for their flexibility in making the deal happen, and to my original editors (Larry Doyle and Laurel Fitch) and managing editor (Alex Wald) for making Squalor happen in the first place.